RONTEL

After my girlfriend left for work this morning, I lay in her bed for an hour looking at the wall.

Fuck, this is really good—I thought.

It was good if you didn't think about doing it as you were doing it.

Sometimes I put my hands up to cover my face.

That made it even better.

*

I went to the bathroom.

There were flakes of my girlfriend's makeup left in the sink.

When I turned on the water to rinse my face, the water carried the flakes down the drain.

And I saw a miniature version of myself surfing on one of the flakes.

The miniature version of myself looked back up at me and smiled, yelling nonsense and pointing at me—then into the drain, laughing and yelling.

And the normal-sized version of myself watched, jealous.

So very jealous.

I put water against my face and rubbed my eyes.

It made me feel better, but only for a few minutes.

Then it stopped.

No, like, it just blended into the terror.

And I decided when it was my turn to be the smaller version of myself riding a flake of makeup down the drain—I'd wave to the normal-sized me and yell "into the terror" before entering the drain, laughing.

*

I encountered my girlfriend's roommate in the hallway.

Her roommate disapproved of me being there when my girlfriend wasn't. We didn't say anything to each other as I went out the door.

Just another person I don't interact with.

*

An hour and twenty minute commute to get back to Uptown.

I walked down Western Avenue to get to the Blue Line train.

Blue Line to Red Line.

Had to get back home.

It was my last day of work at the department store warehouse where I'd been working for the last two years.

And even though it was my last day, I didn't want to be late.

Because then someone would say, "Hey, why are you late."

And I wouldn't lie.

I'd just turn away and avoid eye contact and say, "I'm tired" or something similar.

Something similar like, "I'm (scream in his/her face)."

*

Western Avenue.

Not even summer yet and already hot.

Fuck Western Avenue and fuck Chicago.

Fuck the summer and fuck all these people.

People going to work.

People coming home from work.

People without work.

People going to his/her last day of work.

People without homes.

People just standing there.

People selling drugs.

People trying to buy drugs.

People holding hands.

People with credit cards, keys, and cellphones.

People biking.

People skateboarding.

People walking dogs.

People talking to themselves.

People sleeping underneath doorframes.

People under the Western Bridge, their mattresses between concrete support beams, right next to the street.

People handing out fliers.

People refusing fliers.

People taking fliers then throwing them in the garbage five feet later.

People on parole, cleaning streets and sidewalks.

People sitting on milk crates on the sidewalk, staring.

People with no idea how to spend the day.

People who wished the day was already over.

People whose day was already over.

People.

Hey people.

Suck my dick.

Thought about myself in front of everything.

Thought about the nearly impossible idea that there was this many things and so many more, then endless things between them where they intersect, and mean something different to everyone.

And how everything referenced me.

Me, the most necessary part of all.

No way to think of anything without the idea of me involved.

Involved.

The idea of me.

Each thing needed me.

I didn't need them, but they needed me.

And standing there breathing on the sidewalk, I did my job.

You're welcome, Chicago.

No, I said you're fucking welcome.

And also, suck my dick.

*

On a side street, I saw a kid kicking an apple down the sidewalk.

I watched him, not knowing what else I should be doing.

Not having anything else to do.

I decided I wasn't going to work.

What should I be doing right now—I thought.

Watch the kid kick the apple.

There is nothing that can't be learned from this.

Learn something maybe.

Do that.

Ok, I'll do that, thanks.

I watched the kid kicking the apple, imagining it as my heart.

My heart felt so hurt right then but I didn't know why.

Never knew why I felt so hurt for things I couldn't explain.

Or why feeling hurt was my commitment to others.

Wanting to admit everything that was wrong about me—then hear the things other people noticed and admit to those things too.

Admit to everything.

At least I have that.

Nothing could happen to me that I hadn't already prepared myself to feel.

Fully guarded.

Making it so whatever actually happens, happens easy.

Unafraid.

The kid kicked the apple a few more times—his hands in fists.

Yeah.

Get it.

Kill it.

When the apple rolled to a stop by a fire hydrant, he went up and just stomped it.

Blasted it, really.

Down the block a woman yelled, "Jeffr', get da fuck over here nah!"

The kid stomped the apple twice more with his heel.

The way he stomped the apple was funny.

Balancing himself above it in just the right place to lift his leg and stomp the apple—both hands in fists at his sides, heel stabbing.

"Jeff-REE—get—duffuck—ov'yere nah. Mam'said she gon keel y'ass, Jeffr'."

Jeffrey ran towards her.

I stared at the stomped apple.

What is the normal thing to be doing right now.

What should I be doing.

Having access to any and all options—what was the normal thing to be doing right at that moment, walking down Western Avenue in Chicago at the beginning of an extremely hot summer.

What was the normal thing to be doing, as myself at that moment.

Given all the qualities I embodied and could use to interact with the world, what was the right series of actions to begin taking.

What if the first action to be taken was to return to the stomped apple and keep stomping it.

What if I was supposed to protect the apple.

Or what if it wasn't even normal to be in this very moment, doing what I was doing as this person.

What if I didn't even have the option for something great because I couldn't even return to a situation that allowed it.

I heard a spaceship captain in my head, and he said, "Original route, impossible. We now enter: Total Isolation."

Maybe the right series of actions led me back to where I went wrong and then to a whole new series, but I only had enough energy if I didn't expend a single needless move or thought.

Maybe no series.

Nothing connected.

Blankness responding to my sonar.

No people to talk to.

No signs.

No things.

No, there were things.

But there was no single thing, only things.

And I couldn't get the things to work together.

I'd make like, two or three work, but then I'd realize those two or three things were attached to everything else, which never worked.

Because other things would say, "No, we're not going to work with these things."

And the possibility of mishandling the events of my life or any life was so likely and so final, it stunned me from wanting anything.

Which was terrible because I was always the furthermost moment in time, passing into the next furthermost moment.

Chicago, Illinois.

United States of America.

2012.

The latest in shithead technology.

Breathing, on a street corner.

Endless options, mine.

*

I stopped at a stoplight, where the "DON'T WALK" signal counted down twenty seconds.

Two women talked, sitting on a bus stop bench nearby.

One said, "Now dey trynna gemme for murda." Pointing at where her one eye was missing, she said, "How you gon say a bitch with one eye"—she pointed at her eye, which was open wide—"*one eye*, finna murda someone. I cain even see the motherfuckuh. Hah. Wh'I look like, muh fucking magician?"

The other woman said, "Oh, so issa, like, issa real trial then."

"Yeah, they trynna *get* me," the first one said. "Ain about ta happen like that though, girl. Uh uh."

Other one said, "Issa real trial then." Higher pitch, "*Y'all rilly going to trial?*"

"Yeah," the one-eyed lady said, spitting through her top teeth and looking out at the street. "I hope they'ave them pot-pies at market today. Luh those. Shoo."

"Mm hmm. Me too."

"Them tarkey ones," said the one-eyed woman, clearing her throat. "I'on't like the chicken ones. They be putting that purple chewy shit in thuh."

Both laughed.

I thought about walking up and putting my arms around them.

Then look back and forth between their faces, yelling, "Me too, I love pot-pies haha!"—and continue looking back and forth between their faces.

I just wanted to be close to their faces.

Kiss the one-eyed lady once—a quick kiss on the lips.

Boom.

How do you feel.

I changed you.

You'll remember me.

The thought of me will grow inside you until my head bursts out from the hole in your face and I kiss you again.

Boom.

Lovely faces.

Lovely, lovely faces.

Life is the equation for more and more faces.

Addition.

Everything getting added.

Where the sum doesn't change.

A truly pointless equation where what happens happens and moves you towards the end where you supplement another section of the equation, faceless and weak and irrelevant.

Scary!

The "WALK" signal flashed and I continued down Western.

I put my fingers in my ears and softly said, "Scary," and it sounded loud and bass-heavy in my head.

Then I said, "Uhhh" a few times, my fingers still in my ears.

It was fucking funny.

*

97 degrees out according to a bank LED sign.

Which meant with humidity it was like 110.

I walked on down Western Avenue and found myself changing thoughts rapidly, attempting to stop each one before it happened fully.

Saw thoughts coming at me like little birds on fire, and I dodged or parried each one.

Some I dodged by moving my head to the left or right, some I dodged by lifting my right or left shoulder up enough to deflect them.

Some came fast and some came lazy, undeveloped, and sideways.

Others I ducked under with ease, smiling.

Because few were ever helpful.

Most just recurred and made me feel terrible.

Episodes.

Recycled in my head at frequencies causing great pain and discomfort.

The terrible divide between trying and being ready to try.

The training.

Which never worked because it was never the thing actually happening.

Sweating.

Worried I could never be myself because of always having to account for so much else.

An airplane flew low overhead, heading toward O'Hare.

And I said "Scary" again and the sound of the plane covered it.

And I vividly recalled a scene from a fur-hunting video I saw where a man stepped on the head of a fox/lemur/something and his boot crushed the animal's head and blood came pouring out both nostrils in perfect streams.

*

A block before the Blue Line I passed a tree on the sidewalk.

In the square of dirt around the tree, a dead cat lay on its side.

The carcass was beat the fuck up.

Mouth open.

Eyes gone.

Tail stripped.

The rest of the hair on it looked harshly slicked down in one direction.

First thing I thought was that someone had "peeled out" on top of it—like in a car where you press the gas pedal down while idling, then put the car in gear to make the tires peel off on the ground.

That seemed funny to me—someone "peeling out" on a dead cat.

And for a few seconds, the thought of someone peeling out on a dead cat made me completely lose my mind.

Anybody in Chicago could've robbed me or murdered me or whatever and I wouldn't have known what to do.

Insane!

I turned to watch a person behind me discover the cat carcass.

She looked at it and made a face and then looked back up.

We made eye contact.

I smiled and raised my eyebrows twice in quick succession.

Couldn't stop thinking about someone "peeling out" over a cat carcass.

And how I'd have to watch, even if I closed my eyes to it.

How the mouth of the cat carcass would shake terribly at me as the tire spun.

And how, yeah, it'd be fucking awesome if a magic key came out of the cat's shaking mouth—a magical key that took me on a magical journey and ended up, somehow, with me being born as a baby eagle but like, with the mind I have now (why not).

Nearing the subway entrance, I noticed myself raising my eyebrows twice in succession again, but not to anyone—to the ground, to my feet, to Chicago, Illinois.

My feet look weird—I thought, inhaling my first breath of piss smell from the subway entrance.

*

On the Blue Line towards The Loop, I sat down and took out a granola bar I'd stolen from my girlfriend's roommate.

Her roommate had accused me—to my girlfriend—of eating her food.

Which was untrue.

But then because of how hurt I was by the accusation, I started eating her food.

Yes.

Haha fuck off.

I smiled to myself and stared forward, nodding.

For some reason I kept the granola bar close to me, like I didn't want anyone to see it.

Felt stupid to eat in front of others maybe.

Not sure.

Or no, it was because I kept expecting someone to walk up and say, "You should've brought enough for EV'ryone"—punching me on the "EV" syllable, hard enough to cause a bad cut on my face, and then the granola bar would drop to the floor of the train wherefrom nothing returned—and I'd sit in the seat, one side of my head against the window, hand covering the side badly cut from the punch delivered by a person upset about me not sharing—cowering against the train window holding my battered, cut face, grinding my teeth with my eyes closed.

A few seats down, two kids and their mothers sang the alphabet song.

A lot of people in the car clapped at the end.

Minutes later the kids started singing it again and the moms only half sang and there was less clapping.

I didn't clap either time.

*

I got off the Blue Line train and went down the stairs into the transfer.

In the long, tiled tunnel between the Blue Line and the Red Line, I imagined flames slowly building at each end of the tunnel, with no time or way for me to get out on either end.

So I just stand there screaming and flames fill the tunnel.

Quickly filling the entire tunnel.

You should've brought enough for EV'ryone.

*

People could perform on the platform area between Red Line trains.

Today there was a man singing.

I'd never seen him.

He was wearing a fisherman's hat, two white gloves, and a denim vest with denim shorts.

He sang through a microphone plugged into a small PA speaker by his feet.

The PA speaker loudly amplified a slow drumbeat and bass guitar.

There was a tip jar on the ground.

The singer took a few steps forward.

In front of the speaker stood a little boy who was barely able to walk.

Singer said, "'At's my son, eyr-one. Say hi."

Nobody said hi.

I said hi in my head.

The kid looked two.

He was making unsteady single and double steps in front of the PA speaker, eating a small bag of chips.

The music was so loud but he didn't seem scared.

He just danced, eating chips.

Then he started bouncing up and down, bending at the knees.

Classic baby style.

I felt like turning to the girl next to me and saying, "Ah, *class*ic baby style."

The singer wearing the fisherman's hat and denim vest finished the song.

He breathed hard into the microphone.

He said, "Woo, Chi-town. We g'in too hot. Ish shit too hot. My hands burnin' up on this mic hurr. Damn it."

And he continued to talk in a way that indicated he was delaying.

Then a phone-ringing sound played through the PA speaker.

The singer said, "Oh, ho-don, I'm *so* so sorry Chicago, I gossa take this."

He reached down to the ground and picked up an old housephone receiver, cord dangling.

He had a conversation with his "woman" while his son stared off—not dancing anymore—just staring off with his finger in the side of his mouth.

I watched him.

If he drops the chips, the chips are mine—I thought.

Yeah, take the chips if they fall.

Act like you're going to pick the bag up for him then scurry off like a little bitch, eating the chips in such a way that they fall from your mouth, disgusting.

The singer talked with more excitement.

He said, "Oh baby what was you doing b'fo? I almost hung up on you. Oh—oh you was, you was making a hot beef and uh, bologna sandwich? Oh ok, well, well haha you still coming over t'night? Oh ok good, then make sure you brang me, uh, summa that—" then he yelled, "HOT STUFF."

Which then segued into a song where the lyrics were, "Looking for some hot stuff baby this evening/Looking for some hot stuff, baby, tonight."

The singer thrust his crotch forward once to each syllable in "HOT STUFF."

And for a second his kid looked like he was about to cry—finger in mouth, eyes pinching up.

But then this girl a few years older came and danced with him.

And he smiled and danced with her, taking his finger out of his mouth.

Accidentally dropped the chips.

A group of kids all wearing the same high school gym uniforms walked up, cheering.

Other people gathered too.

I moved forward to get a better view.

This kid is so awesome—I thought.

And will one day grow to be a man.

Will one day eat more chips.

The song ended with a lot of chime sounds and then the singer was wiping his head with a bandana, foot up on the PA speaker.

His son continued dancing even though there was no more music.

Just bending up and down at the knees.

People cheered.

One guy had his hand up to his mouth, yelling, "Ooh ooh." He slapped his leg a little. "Shit," he said. "Aw shit. Check out dude. Dude crazy."

Someone else said, "Too cray. He bout ta fall out."

Everyone was laughing and cheering.

I stood there smiling.

Down the platform a man in a fabric hotdog suit was handing out coupons.

No one talked to him.

Something about the man in the fabric hotdog suit bothered me.

But I didn't know what.

I thought—hotdog man, I'ma fucking get you, don't worry.

"Uh oh," someone said. "Little dude getting fierce nah."

The kid's pace had increased.

Someone turned to me and hit my arm and said, "You seeing this. This motherfucker—he a mobsta."

Someone next to him said, "*This* dude lethal."

"Yeah this dude is lethal," I said, not that loud.

Sometimes I would just repeat things to people as a way to allow the conversation to keep going.

By saying the same thing the person just said, I'd sustain the thought, rather than interrupt it with whatever I had to add, which probably wasn't anything I wanted to add.

"*Lethal*," the person said again. "Somebody arrest'zis lil nigga."

His friends laughed.

The singer said, "You have the right to remain LEEEEEEETHAL."

Someone from the crowd yelled, "Chi-town LETHal!"

Other people yelled.

The kid put his finger in his mouth again, still dancing.

Someone else said, "Oooh, he tryn some sexy shit now."

"He's lethal," I said again, looking at the ground a little, searching for the chips.

Someone said, "Them little legs is all like jellyfish."

The singer started another song and people watched his son dance a little longer before trains arrived and everyone boarded.

The guy in the hotdog suit, still there.

He was in a conversation now, holding out a coupon pamphlet.

The person hadn't taken it.

Yes, hotdog man.

Yes.

Yes, do this.

Do this dirt, my man.

Make them take the pamphlet.

Make them realize they want it.

The train departed, me nodding my head and watching hotdog man through a window.

And right then, I wanted to know that someone in the train was watching me—and could hear me—so I could turn and stare straight forward and say, "Everything is in place for the lunar harvest"—then sit down and continue staring straightforward, smiling.

*

There was a day-old newspaper on the seat next to me.

A small daily paper.

It had stories about what celebrities ate at what Chicago restaurants.

It told people what movies to see and what shows to watch and what books to read and what to do for fun.

It had "where to drink" suggestions that referenced "cool bars/city spots" for the white people in the city who all moved here together after college.

The daily paper also had "debate" articles between staff writers who were trying to be funny/cute.

The debates would be like, "Is it ok to date someone who hates your best friend."

Or: "What's the code for roommate bathroom sharing."

Or: "Are moustaches cool."

Or: "Hash browns or fruit for breakfast."

Today I read the crime blotter.

I liked the crime blotter.

The only place in the newspaper where they just stated facts about something that happened without trying to make it fun.

My favorite crime blotter ever was: "Man in Uptown beats upstairs neighbor then drags her to the basement and sets her on fire."

Today there were four news items in the crime blotter.

One was about a man forcing children into his car and then molesting them in an alley.

The next was about a man raping a child who attended the daycare his wife ran at home.

Next one about a man stabbing his doctor then trying to rape her.

Next one about a man who died in an alley after being stabbed in the throat "repeatedly."

I looked up from the paper and out the window.

Felt like my face was the ugliest melt ever at that point.

Like, the worst.

I felt so stupid-looking.

Always felt ugly and stupid on the train.

Like almost, sagged.

Sagged out.

Sagged out and sorry.

Horrific.

Sorry I'm so saggy, but I'm sagged out and sorry.

Suck my dick—I thought, addressing myself.

The train was underground.

I stared at the tunnel wall, and its lighting.

Thought about stabbing someone in the throat repeatedly.

Is there any way to do it except repeatedly.

Could it really stop after one stab.

I thought about stabbing someone once then just standing there.

Seemed like that would be worse.

What would I do just standing there after the first stab.

Would I talk to the victim.

If they said something to me, I feel like I'd definitely respond.

So I'd either have to stand there to make sure the person died or stab them repeatedly to ensure it.

Also, seemed like if I stabbed once then paused, it would be hard to get back into it.

It'd be like sweating in a shirt, then taking the shirt off and putting it back on like, fifteen minutes later.

So yeah. Repeatedly.

Once seemed cruel.

That would be the worst thing to read: 'Man stabbed in throat once, dies in alley over an extended period of time.'

Just get it done—I thought, looking back into the train car.

Finish everything you start.

Finish yourself.

I'ma finish you, Chicago—I thought, feeling pleasure in my testicles from the shaking of the train.

*

At the other end of the train car there was a kid in a mechanized wheelchair device.

He had his thumb in his mouth.

He had a really serious look on his face.

An older woman stood behind him with her hands on the wheelchair.

On the left armrest of the wheelchair device there was a keyboard attached to something.

We made eye contact.

Felt like I was looking at myself.

The misery.

With the hand of the thumb in his mouth, he waved by bending all four fingers down and up and down and up.

The way he did it seemed like it was happening real slow.

Felt so friendly too.

Like we knew each other.

The misery.

I looked at him and tried to silently communicate, "This, sucks."

But I couldn't tell if it worked.

Couldn't tell if I'd thought, "This, sucks" or if the kid in the wheelchair put the thought inside my head.

That would be terrible.

I stared at him and thought—No, you will NOT control me.

He continued sucking his thumb, the thumb that should've been over the keyboard controls of his wheelchair.

His dashboard.

Are you my space captain.

When does it end.

And where.

Am I brave enough.

I looked back at the newspaper.

I liked to have a newspaper on the train so no one would talk me.

It wasn't the only guard against interaction, but definitely the best.

Staring at a newspaper for a long time seemed normal—but staring at any other object on the train for a long period didn't.

If you just stared at something without words on it, someone would eventually fuck with you.

They're here to fuck with me—I thought.

The tension of feeling perfectly fine with just staring at anything, versus other people fucking with you.

The tension.

Such bad tension!

Let me show you how a real man endures bad tension.

Been doing that a lot lately, adding "Let me show you how a real man (does something)" to a lot of my thoughts or conversations.

Like, yesterday my girlfriend went to walk across the street before we had a walk signal and I held her back and said, "Let me show you how a real man obeys traffic law."

In the newspaper there was one last item in the crime blotter, presented in the form of a giant quote with the story beneath.

The quote was from someone who witnessed a stabbing outside a bar in Rogers Park.

The quote read: "Yeah this guy came up, and was going to give him (the victim) a hug, and then he (attacker) says, 'Hey, what's up' and stabbed him in the back."

So—someone randomly approached someone else outside a bar and said, "Hey what's up," then offered a hug, then stabbed the person as the hug was accepted.

My heavens.

I sat there terrified.

Why would anyone accept some random hug.

I'd never accepted a random hug in my life.

And never would!

Actually no.

What the fuck.

Who am I to deny.

I'd take the first one offered by anyone right now—even if I saw the person holding a giant knife behind his/her back.

Even if the person ended up stabbing me, I'd take a deep breath and put my mouth by his or her ear and say, "I knew you'd do this. I knew it, sweetheart. And, well I still thank you for the hug."

I turned the page.

There was an article about a television show where people competed by losing weight.

I closed the newspaper and put it on the ground.

Welcome to your new home.

*

The train made a stop at Damen Street and the kid in the mechanized wheelchair exited, pushed out by his mother.

Thumb in his mouth still.

He did the same wave—keeping his eyes forward.

Pushed away, waving.

Signaling, "Laaaaater, asshole."

And I realized that part of my problem was I visibly resembled an adult.

But never became one.

People viewed me as an adult but I was just shit.

I always expected adulthood to happen, to make, like, a popping or dinging sound when it did.

But no.

Newly twenty-nine years old and nowhere near anything different than ever before.

Not even youthful.

Just the same pile, moving around.

Shifting anxieties—moving a pile of lead around to different areas of the same giant bare room.

To then realize I've become the pile.

The truth.

All just one time period.

One big now.

No adulthood.

Rapidly moving away from any kind of connection.

I could imagine borders around periods of my life to make it seem like I'd become a different person, but that would just be a failure to see there was no more changing or nearness of change as the person on either side of those imagined borders.

Not sure.

Not important.

Not going to shower today. (Third day in a row, yeah!)

What if I just donated all my organs and everything useful about me right now, even the few good thoughts I'd had.

What if I walked into a hospital and said, "I'm going to kill myself anyway, you want my shit or not, come on"—then wait a second and say, "Come on, talk to me talk to me let's go."

I saw myself entering the hospital and confidently walking up to the front desk, resting my elbow on the counter.

"Yeah, come on, let's see a doctor, sweetheart," I'd say, regardless of the front desk worker's gender—and I'd be snapping. "Come on come on." Then, even if the employee was talking to me, say, "Talk to me here, come on."

Let me show you how a real man sits on the train and stares, uninterested, briefly able to visualize his body hollowed out of all its operative points.

*

In a different row of seating an old man sat with the back of his skull against the metal headrest bar, waking up with each bump.

He kept trying to resist sleep but would then fall asleep.

Yes, it's ok, old man.

Fall asleep.

You've earned it.

It's time to sleep.

Sleep time.

Be calm.

I am with you.

Dream about us holding hands—floating up and up and up and yelling and laughing the whole time.

Dream about me performing surgery on you, salting your beating heart (why not).

The old man kept waking up and going to sleep.

Just sleep.

You're not missing anything.

I'll wake you up if something happens.

I'll tell you when to get off the train.

We won't forget your stop.

I sat there thinking about which of his bones I could probably break with my bare hands.

I compiled a list.

Arrived at the Wilson Street stop in Uptown Chicago.

And yeah if people had access to my thoughts and feelings, I'd be asked to live on a rock in outer space—one with a long tether to a building in Chicago if any of my friends (just kidding) wanted to come visit.

*

Going through the turnstile, I heard two people by the ticket machine.

One said, "—and really, that's the bottom line."

I wanted to ask what the bottom line was since I'd missed that part.

Hadn't heard what he said right before it.

Because if I knew where the bottom line was, it'd be easy to avoid it, or jump over it, or do whatever you do to it.

*

Exiting out onto the street in hundred degree weather, I got shot in the face and died.

Didn't even really hear it because my head was immediately all over the sidewalk.

No.

That didn't happen.

I just walked down the street, sweating.

Passed an old man, bald but with long hair on the sides and back.

He had one arm.

Hunched over and limping down the sidewalk, smoking a hand-rolled cigarette.

Saying, "Buhhhhgghhhnnnnn—ahhhhhmmhh."

That was the first person I saw in Uptown this morning.

*

Next I saw an old woman sitting on the single step to an apartment building, right along the sidewalk.

She wore a winter coat in the hundred degree heat.

She sat with her knees together, feet spread.

She had her head down, face to her palms.

The hair on the back of her head stuck up in spikes like it'd been rubbed a lot until it knotted together.

I could see her scalp.

She looked up at me.

The wind made her hair float around her head for a few seconds and she said, "Fif-ty cents," real slow.

She only had the front four teeth on the top and bottom of her mouth and they looked like they were covered in caramel. "Fif-ty cents," the teeth slowly came together like insect pincers.

I thought—Summer is weird because I always forget that it happens and what it's like when it does happen and then it happens and I remember.

Always surprisingly unique and lovely.

This summer I'm going to kill myself—I thought.

And felt confident I would.

And confidence is all I need—I thought.

*

Honestly though, at some point, it would be my time to get shot.

Every couple days/weeks someone got shot in the area.

I awaited it eagerly.

It would define me.

Definition: Shithead shot dead on the street, found with receipt from a four dollar and fifty-three cents purchase at a gas station in his pocket.

Sometimes I'd be walking down the street and get a sense that it was about to happen.

That it was my day.

That the universe had arranged itself perfectly around this very day, for me to get shot.

That the universe's creation supported one final moment in a long series of other seemingly important moments, and it involved bullets in my head and chest.

And all I'd have to do is relax myself and allow the bullets into my body.

Focus my mind on it happening.

Sustain the focus and let it finish.

I'd take the first shot, the next shot, multiple shots, spreading across my chest in a series of bloody holes.

And no disagreement.

I'd be no different.

Just put my hands over the bloody holes in my shirt and say, "Hey, you ruined my shirt man."

Bleeding to death.

Like to get me some of that action.

"Like to get me some of that action" was a phrase I recently started using.

I started saying it after I saw this cop the other day.

I wanted to ask the cop how much money was made through drugs every year in Chicago—then when he approximated something,

I was going to slap my hands together and rub them a little, saying, "Like to get me some of *that* action."

*

Out front of the apartment building that shares an alley with mine, my friend(?) the maintenance man dragged two giant bags of garbage, sweating.

He said, "Wassap, my frent."

He looked at both bags of garbage.

"Too metch," he said. "Too metch garbetch. S'too hot for garbetch I'm taking outsite, my man."

He was shrugging and smiling too.

I slapped my hands together and said, "Like to get me some of *that* action."

He laughed, gesturing towards me with the garbage again.

He pretty much always laughed no matter what I said.

Which is a weird thing to repeatedly happen between two people.

Because sometimes the things I said didn't warrant laughter (I think) and it was always a little stunning and depressing.

Can't help that it felt that way, but it did.

It always did.

Fated to feel certain ways.

All my fates outlived—I thought.

Tired all the time.

*

I went through the alley after holding the dumpster lids open for the maintenance man.

Someone had left a microwave out.

There was a handwritten note on a ripped piece of paper taped to the microwave.

The note read, "I still work!"

I still work—I thought.

I still work, motherfucker.

Which one of you motherfuckers thought I stopped working.
Wait.
Wait no.
Who thought I stopped working.
Oh no no.
Because I didn't.
No.
I never stopped working.
You thought I stopped.
You *actually* thought that.
And went on with your lives.
You still worked, thinking I didn't.
But I do still work.
I still work and I want you to know that.

*

Two teenagers came up on skateboards as I exited the alley by my building.

They asked me to watch them do tricks and we talked about skateboarding while I watched them miss/not do tricks correctly.

The more incorrectly each trick was done, the more I had to watch again—the more they made sure I was watching.

I watched a lot of tricks then said thank you and goodbye and they skated away.

On the door to my apartment building, there was a handwritten note taped to the glass:

"Need help. L(*scratched out letter*)ost dog on Malden St. I was on ground having seasure. Had leash and colar too. Call 773 --- ----."

I saw myself in the window of the front door as I went in.

My face looked sunk.

I still work.

I still work!

*

I lived with my brother.

Our apartment was two studio apartments connected.

He lived in one studio, with its own door.

I lived in a sectioned off area of the second studio, in a four feet by eight feet room divided by a bedsheet staplegunned to the ceiling and hung to the floor.

What a life!

When I got back today, my brother was sitting on our ripped and broken couch playing a hockey videogame from 1997.

He'd recently been fired, receiving unemployment.

Rontel lay on the armrest of the couch, holding the corner with his front legs like a gargoyle.

He kept blinking like he was going to fall asleep.

He went to meow but no sound came out.

He never really meowed at all.

He'd just look at me and open his mouth—with a dry clicking from his lips.

My brother paused the videogame.

"I got a new one, man," he said, setting down his controller.

He picked up Rontel.

He made Rontel hold out his paw like Rontel wanted to shake hands with me.

"Come on man, shake," my brother said, waving Rontel's paw.

I said, "Hey, you got it," holding out my hand to shake hands with Rontel.

Then my brother pulled Rontel's paw back.

In the same motion, he made the paw slick back the hair on top of Rontel's head—and flicked the paw forward like Rontel was flicking the grease from his hair at me.

The whole time Rontel just stared forward, slowly going to sleep.

My brother put Rontel's paws on Rontel's belly and made Rontel laugh like, "ohh ohh ohh"—doing the laughs for him—moving paws up and down his belly.

"You motherfucker," I said. "You sexy, motherfucker."

My brother dropped Rontel, slapped his hands together to get the hair off.

Rontel landed on his paws and shook his head a little, paused, shook his head a little more, then came over to rub his head on my legs.

First he just brushed his head as he walked past.

Then he came back around and put his forehead against my leg and did half a rotation and kept his head there.

Then in the opposite direction.

"We should shave his head again," my brother said, returning to the videogame.

Last year we shaved Rontel's head.

Only his head, not the rest of his body.

It looked really weird.

His head/skull was extremely small underneath the hair.

Made him look like a bug or an alien.

Rontel liked it though.

He went around rubbing his head on things more.

He'd rub his head back and forth on the corner of a wall for ten minutes without stopping.

And the way he'd shut his eyes while doing it seemed to convey deeper satisfaction as opposed to when his hair was normal length.

My brother said, "This time we need to shave lines into him so it looks like he's wearing a shirt or some shit." Then he yelled "fuck" at the TV.

He twisted the controller a little, crackling sounds.

Then he motioned towards the other controller with his foot.

"Oh, I'll watch," I said.

But he motioned to the controller again, scratching the side of his head really hard.

Usually I'd just sit there watching him play, as I silently terrified myself with bad thoughts, waiting to feel tired.

But he needed me.

I was the top scorer in the game.

So I sat down on the floor and played.

We were the Chicago Blackhawks.

Rontel jumped back onto the arm of the couch and lay like a gargoyle.

I put my head against the arm of the couch and Rontel licked the back of my neck twice.

While the game reset, my brother said, "Oh man, this guy I saw coming home the other night. There was this guy with a Bears coat on and a thick moustache with big ass sunglasses, like the mirrored kind. We were on the Green Line train. He was so fucking drunk. And he showed me a long, like, some kind of case he was carrying. It looked like it was for a pool cue maybe."

For some reason, I waved my hand dismissively and—using a voice I'd never used—said, "Ah, those no-good stinkin drunks." Then, using the same voice, I said, "I hates them no good stinking juh-runks."

It seemed insane.

I felt fully insane for a few seconds.

Kept waving my hand downward, dismissively, saying, "Bah."

Rontel was making pigeon-sounds on the arm of the couch behind me, licking my neck.

My brother didn't say anything.

"So what about the guy," I said. "He was just drunk and had a pool cue bag."

"No. He was like, laughing, and he looked at me and smiled and pointed at the case. Then he goes, 'Guess'w's in the bag.' I told him I didn't know. Then he asked me to guess what was in the bag a few more times. Kept smiling every time I told him I didn't know. Finally, he's like, 'S'rattlesnake. Iced'em wit my bir hands.' Then he was like, 'D'I'iced a rattler wit my bir hands.' He kept saying that. 'D'I'iced him.'"

"Iced him," I said.

"'D'I'iced'em.' Like, 'I iced him.'"

I kept imagining a man lunging at the ground with his bare hands in the classic "strangling pose," missing a few times, groaning each miss, but then capturing the rattlesnake and icing it.

Really icing it.

I thought—These are the days when man ices the rattlesnake.

My brother slicked Rontel's hair back with his bare left foot.

"I'ma ice you with my bare hands, Rontel," he said.

"Give him the business," I said.

My brother said, "Give him the fucking business."

"Giving him the business" was a phrase we'd been using.

It was one of the programmed sayings in the hockey videogame from 1997.

If someone got hit hard in the game, the announcer might say, "Ooooh, he *gives him the business.*"

My brother said, "S'rattler"—using the guy's voice. "D'I'iced him." Then he leaned to the other end of the couch and head-butted Rontel, saying, "Hyuhh, hyuhh" with each head-butt.

Every time my brother's head hit Rontel's head, there was a small hollow sound.

The small hollow sound was both funny and sad.

Rontel just lay there blinking.

If the head-butt was especially hard he'd close his eyes, his ears down all the way.

"He gives him the business," I said, feeling like what I really wanted was to meet a new woman and develop romantic feelings towards her and have sex with her once, then repeat that many more times with others and call it a life.

No, jump out a high window and call it a life.

"Hyuhh, hyuhh."

My brother used the videogame announcer voice and said, "Ooh, giving him the business," as he rapidly head-butted Rontel.

Rontel just lay there clenching his eyes shut, ears down.

My brother stopped.

"Shit," he said, trying to focus.

He looked unsteady.

Then he said, "Hyuhh, hyuhh" real fast and head-butted Rontel twice more. "All right, no more."

Our game began.

My brother always just selected this one really big player and then went around knocking people over while I scored goals.

It was funny to see him needlessly hitting people.

The sounds were funny too.

Like, "Urgh" and "Bwuh."

One sounded like, "Hyuhh."

Sometimes my brother would just skate around a player he knocked over, and then knock him over again when he got up.

Over and over.

"The violence," I said, watching a replay where my brother's player elbowed someone in the face and injured him for the rest of the season.

We were already up 3-1.

I'd scored three wonderful goals.

Finesse.

"Fucking finesse," I said. "Violent finesse, motherfucker."

"Who want that violence," my brother said.

Upstairs, people screamed at each other.

There were stomping sounds and screaming.

Then—while the game was showing a replay of my brother hitting someone into the opposing team's bench area—I looked across the room, out the window.

Across the courtyard—in another second story apartment—a slightly overweight woman showered.

I could see her through the bathroom window.

Every apartment in the building had a window in the shower.

She looked good.

Her chubby shoulders and back were wet.

I want to fuck you so hard—I thought.

Then I heard an audience in my head and they all said, "How hard!"

But I didn't answer.

Baby, I don't even know how hard I want to fuck you.

Baby, I'm scoring goals, I don't have a job, I don't have a future, I'm NO-good, hm.

And I imagined myself telling her that, rubbing my chin thoughtfully and staring at her thighs.

The attraction was not entirely sexual though.

Like—maybe if I were in that shower with her—I'd just rest my forehead on her shoulder while the water hit us both.

Is that sexual.

Actually that seems sexual.

Maybe it *is* sexual!

I scored another goal.

It was extremely impressive.

Not even going to describe it because I already know I could never do that.

Anyone witnessing it would be impressed though.

I looked at Rontel and thought about how pretty he was.

How much I loved him.

How, actually no, if he died it probably wouldn't affect me.

Like, there was nothing to be taken from me that would affect me.

Like, I'd trained myself to feel no harm.

True sadness.

Let me show you how a real man endures true sadness.

When I focused on the game, my brother knocked someone over and then I skated up to the fallen player and tried to shoot the puck into his face.

It was a thing me and my brother always tried to do.

He'd knock someone over then I'd skate up and try to shoot the puck at the fallen player's face.

This time the puck went over the player's head and into the crowd.

My brother laughed.

I liked making him laugh.

"So close," he said. Then he said, "You no-good stinkin' drunk" and slapped just the very tip of Rontel's ear.

The sound was "fip."

The videogame showed multiple replays of the guy lying on the ice, as the puck just slightly missed hitting his face.

Seemed so brutal.

I briefly entertained the idea of dying a humorously needless death, like from something people get routinely treated by doctors, something simple.

Like, a mole getting too big and becoming skin cancer.

A simple infected blister, anything.

Gimme something—I thought.

Rabies.

Rabies, of course, was the ultimate.

The one to achieve.

I looked at Rontel.

I grabbed his ear tip with my forefinger and thumb and "sizzled" his ear.

An "Ear Sizzle."

Ear Sizzle: When you grab his ear by the tip, and gently (gently!) make the "money" motion with your forefinger and thumb, creating a "sizzling" sound when the hair rubs the soft part of his ear.

"Give him the business," my brother said.

I continued sizzling Rontel's ear.

Rontel's eyes blinked almost closed and his mouth hung open a little.

I got Rontel for free when a past roommate brought home a cat from some farm and the cat was pregnant.

Few weeks later, she gave birth to four kittens...and one half-human/half-kitten.

No.

Just four kittens.

I kept one of the kittens and named him Rontel (I'd been on the bus one time and heard some lady on her phone, yelling, "I ah-ready tol'joo Rontel, get the fuck off the muffucking TV, don't be standing on that muffucking TV, it can't hol'jo ass, stupit muffucker.")

Rontel.

Rontel jumped off the armrest of the couch and went into his enclosed plastic litterbox.

Just his head showed through the plastic entrance.

I imagined him in a rocketship.

And the rocketship ascended through the ceiling of the apartment—the ceiling of the next one—the roof of the apartment building—all the clouds in the way—through stretches of space—to some kind of gigantic glowing amoeba, where Rontel jetpacks out of his spaceship into the amoeba—where getting digested is the last and only holy experience of life—where Rontel dies, reincarnated as my mind at present.

I don't know, it's like, there's no relationship with anyone outside of yourself, at all, ever.

My brother said, "Hey do you want to go to the post office with me."

I said yes, that I wanted to go to the post office with him.

*

So I didn't go to work then.

But I called off, like an adult.

The boss told me if I ever needed a job again I could call.

I thanked him and ended the call.

Had to conserve the minutes on my shitty prepaid phone.

I got this shitty prepaid phone after not having a phone for over a year.

The screen on my shitty prepaid phone had no light—because I answered it in the shower one time—so now I had to hold it sideways up to a light to read things on it.

I bought it when I still worked at the department store.

The guy who worked the phone section at the time wasn't helpful.

So I kept asking basic questions about phones.

"Come on man," he said, after I'd used the phrase "telephoning device" for the third time.

"I just, don't know anything about phones," I said, smiling.

I felt so vulnerable.

Thought he would help.

Thought he would make things better.

Luis, help me.

Luis, please.

I said, "So is this one good then. Or no."

He put one hand in the other and clicked his teeth. Said, "Man, they all pretty much the same. They do basic shit, man."

"And this one comes with the full numerical keyboard—I get all numbers," I said, splaying my fingers out over the model phone attached to a small piece of pressboard.

He said, "There's a manual with each one on how to use it and what it does, man. You can go on the internet and shit but it looks like a fucking videogame from the 80s and it barely works—but yeah it does *some* shit."

"And now, is this the classic 'Ear to the top/mouth to the bottom' type of phoning device."

He started helping someone else.

I wanted to ask if I had to dial the number then hit some kind of "send" button, or if just dialing the number correctly would send the call.

The phone cost twenty dollars and then I had to buy a plastic card with minutes.

It was like, a fun thing to watch my time run out.

It gave my life a certain urgency that—if searched—would be hiding its own version of, "No, not yet."

The first thing I did after entering the minutes was send my brother a message.

I walked out of the store and stood on the sidewalk.

Sent my brother a message that read: "This is my new phone number: (phone number)...you...fucking bitch."

He sent back: "Haha you got a phone. You're stupid."

*

First night I had the shitty prepaid phone, I lay on the floor of my room, trying to sleep.

My brother and I had just moved in together and didn't have electricity for almost three weeks during that summer's heatwave.

All I'd done for days was sweat and work and take showers where I'd sweat during the shower.

I lay on the slightly cooler floor of my room, crumbs and cat hair all over my naked sweating ass.

I thought—This is the end of something but I'm not sure what.

Then my shitty prepaid phone vibrated.

I checked it.

I pressed a button to receive the message.

Half a minute, subtracted.

The subtraction was done on the screen of the phone.

It showed how many minutes were being subtracted, then showed the remaining total.

Half a minute for a text message.

Full minute for each minute of talking.

A countdown.

An equation.

Death.

The end of my maniac youth.

Extinction.

My face, burnt black against my skull.

World peace times infinity.

I read the message.

It wasn't from my brother and I hadn't given anyone else the number.

The message was: "Hey man, you going to the post-production party??"

Post-production party.

I thought—What if I'm dead and this is an ambassador to an afterlife, and there are many afterlives and it's up to me to select the right one.

I sent back: "Who is this."

Subtract half a minute.

The person sent: "Dude it's Wisnieski."

Half a minute less.

Who's Wisnieski.

I don't know Wisnieski.

But, it was him.

It was really him.

Wisnieski goddamn it.

Me: "Oh hey man, how are you."

Wisnieski: "Good, just seeing how you were getting to the post-production party at Alex's."

"Wait, Alex is having a party????"

"Yeah he didn't tell you. Haha"

"No man. What's up with Alex is he mad at me."

"Shit, I don't think so. You think so?"
"Sometimes with Alex...you just don't know."
"Haha. For real yeah. You coming then?"
Me: "Wisnieski, how are you. Are you ok."
"What. I'm good, why."
"Wisnieski, I mean, are we good. Did I do something."
A few minutes passed without a response.
I started sending, "Are we good" over and over.
My minutes, vanishing.
Drying up.
I'm dying—I thought.
Dying!
Oh Wisnieski, help me!
Please fucking help me.
Me: "Wiskieski, just tell me. We used to be so good man. It was me and you. Just me and ol' Wisnieski. What now."
Minutes passed.
Wisnieski: "Who the fuck is this."
Me: "It's Wisnieski dude."
And I lay there in the dark, waiting for Wisnieski to respond.
To tell me we were all right.
But he never did.
No.
Wisnieski.
What happened.
Where did you go.
I'm never going to get to the post-production party—I thought.
I'll never make it.
Never!
And I spun the shitty phone around on the floor, sweating.
When I looked at the alarm clock, the time changed from 11:52 p.m. to 11:53 p.m.
Somehow it was the worst feeling ever, to watch that happen.
The end of something, but I didn't know what.
Just, the worst.

*

My brother and I walked to the post office.

He had to mail out something for a minor league baseball team.

A few years ago, he signed up for a minor league baseball team's mailing list, under the name Clive Jackson.

Clive Jackson.

He wrote that name on a mailing list and the team started mailing him things: reminders about ticket deals, "free (something)" days, and other things.

Each newsletter or flier always had, "Greetings" (which was typed in the same font as the rest of the letter) then, (in a bigger less defined font), "...Clive!"

Today my brother had to mail out a raffle ticket entry for Clive, with the possibility of winning a duffel bag that had the team's logo on it.

Walking back from the post office—through the hot shitty sidewalks, gang territory, through people, bicyclists, joggers, men selling ice cream off bikes, walkers and standers—we discussed what could be kept inside the duffel bag, *if* Clive Jackson won it.

Ultimately, we agreed the best use for the duffel bag would be zipping up Rontel in it—only up to his chin so his face was exposed—then cutting out four holes for his limbs, which, being too short, would be supplemented by hydraulic(?) mechanical(?) limbs that he could operate with his mind (after we shave his head again and implant what we agreed would be "electrodes or like—").

"I like Clive's chances," my brother said, wringing his hands as we entered an alley.

People had begun throwing out things in the alleys, preparing for moves.

April and August were the moving months.

"Is it April or August," I said.

My brother said, "It's May."

I imagined Rontel operating his duffel bag mechanical limb suit around the apartment.

Would I like him more, less, or the same.

Seemed like I loved him too much to ever think anything different about him.

I was so in love with him.

I imagined him slowly walking around the apartment in his new bionic(?) suit—his artificial limbs making tszoo tszoo sounds and then he starts bumping into the wall over and over and when I get home I find him asleep in the suit, still bumping against the wall, tszoo tszoo sounds.

My brother said something, but I'd been distracted by a nice flower in someone's back yard.

Wanted to pick it for my girlfriend.

Then I realized she might be sad I killed it.

Seemed like something she'd get sad about.

Maybe not.

I could just say, "Here, I killed this for you."

As in, "Of course I would kill something for you."

As in, "Everything is potentially your gift."

My brother and I were both sweating.

"*Kill* you," I said, kicking rocks against someone's garage.

Realized I'd been thinking, "Kill you," about nothing in particular.

Randomly.

Like I don't even know if I'm talking to myself or someone's telling me that or whatever.

Which at first was scary.

Then I realized I did it to preserve myself in some way and it became comfortable.

I kicked some more rocks against a chainlink fence.

Both my hands in fists.

A part of the city skyline was visible over garages and loading docks.

Kill you—I thought.

My brother said, "All I ate today was a bag of jelly beans and some pretzels."

I said, "'All I Ate Today Was Some Pussy' seems like the name of a mix cd someone around here would try to sell you."

My brother said, "All I Ate Today Was Pussy, And Also A Bag Of

Jellybeans And Some Pretzels."

I didn't say anything.

Felt like I should.

But I didn't.

He said, "That's a better name, don't you think."

Then he punched a branch that hung over someone's fence and kicked some rocks.

One of the rocks hit a metal garbage can, which scared a bird out from a bush up into the air.

The fucking business.

*

Back at our building, my brother went upstairs but I saw Enrique in the hallway and he invited me in.

Enrique was my friend from the warehouse where I used to work.

He had an at-all-times transparent sexual interest in me.

He once told me that if I were gay he'd never let a man like me go—a man "who looks and acts like a man."

Today he said, "Oh god, you look shitty. Ugh, I have air conditioning, come in, come in."

Inside, his roommate sat at the kitchen table with his legs crossed, looking angry.

His roommate was really funny.

Big Moms.

Big Moms smiled and winked when he saw me.

He worked at the store with us for like, two months, then got fired when a customer called him a "faggot" and he slapped the customer (like slapped the customer down).

We called him "Big Moms" because he was physically big and also he was the meanest person in the world.

The *whole world!*

Nice to me, but mean to everyone else.

He liked being mean.

I remember him making a girl cry at work once when he raised his hand and looked up towards the ceiling with his face excited, and said, "Bitch, you (pointing at her with his gigantic hand) need to relax, I can smell that vagina through your pants, honey."

He just liked to be mean.

He also liked to fabricate things.

He said shit like: "Rainwater actually has more minerals and nutrients or whatever than bottled water, and potassium too."

Or: "If everyone just didn't buy gasoline for one hour—one hour—all at the same time—then the oil companies would all have to shut down and we'd own those fuckers, you could buy a company for a dollar."

He would just make claims.

Like, "You do know that every time you buy blueberries, it goes to the fucking Mormons."

Seemed so weird for him to be angry and serious about something he made up.

At first I didn't react to whatever he'd say or I'd ask him where he learned whatever he just said.

Then I learned it was better to agree with/encourage him.

Validate him somehow.

Something.

"Yeah you're right about those *fucking* oil companies."

Or: "No, I didn't know yogurt has the same calcium as dandelions, cool. Looks like it's dandelions for me! Fuck yogurt!"

Or: "I guess that makes sense, there aren't many mosquitoes this year because less people are getting the flu and there's less construction, hm. Interesting."

Sometimes it was best to just review things he said.

When I walked in today and squatted in the livingroom, Big Moms said, "Hey you" then nodded towards Enrique and said, "What are you doing with the gayest, most Puerto Rican-iest nerd in fucking Chicago."

Outside of work at the warehouse, Enrique owned a small share of a game store where people gathered to play boardgames and talk about videogames and play live-action games where you act like a wizard or knight or mythical creature.

"Oh *fuck off*," Enrique said. Then he leaned against the counter by the kitchen sink and said, "Ugh, I shouldn't have shown your friend I could put my legs behind my head last night. It's already like throwing a penny down the wishing well down there."

Big Moms smiled and said, "I heard."

I said, "I don't show people I can do that until the sixth time I see them. That's when I pull them aside and say, 'Hey just so you know I can do this,' then put both my legs behind my head."

"Oh *shit*," Enrique said, slapping his face. "Forgot I got a Gaymers meeting tonight."

Gaymers: A club for gay men who liked playing boardgames.

Enrique told me since he was considered a more attractive gay gamer than most—he was called a "unicorn."

When he told me that, I said, "Well I'm very happy to be friends with a unicorn."

He said, "I don't even want to go, I just want to sit here and eat an entire pizza and feel like fucking shit."

"Speaking of anal," Big Moms said, smiling at me. "Whaaaaaat about (girl who worked at store with us)?"

Enrique leaned forward off the counter and said, "What about her."

Big Moms then communicated a rumor he'd heard from someone who worked at the store that I'd had anal sex with (girl who worked at store).

Enrique made a shocked face.

"That's true," I said.

Enrique yelled, "Aw," then said, "You dirty bitch. You're a dirty no good *sucia,* bitch."

He always got jealous.

"She asked," I said.

"Did you use lube or spit," he said, adjusting his glasses and smiling.

I said, "Lube one time, then after that, nothing," and I assumed a louder, more aggressive tone and rubbed my hands and said, "I'd just put it in front first to get slicked, see."

"Spit is for love," Enrique said, making a face and staring off.

Big Moms said, "So, how about your new girl."

"What do you mean," I said. "I don't think it will happen with her."

He said, "Has she ever played with herself in that area, like used a dildo on herself?"

"Or three to five fingers," Enrique said, scratching his shin with the heel of his foot.

"I don't think so," I said. "I don't think it's happening. One thing though," I said, pointing at both of them as I stood up, "I'm not going to rest until I get you no-good homos out of my goddamn building."

Big Moms said, "Honey, the 'mos own this part of town—sorry."

And he pointed up into the air, looking up at the ceiling and rotating his head.

Big Moms.

I love you, you stupid ass.

I sang a few lines of a song I made up that had the lyrics "... like a penny down a wishing well," and Enrique and Big Moms were already humming backup as I went to leave.

Enrique said, "Wait, help me order a pizza so I can eat the whole thing and feel like shit. I can't do this shit." He sat down by the computer, clicked on a number of things and typed random keys and made noise by hitting things. "How the fuck do you do this."

I went over to help him.

He was on an internet page for a pizza place.

"You want me to help you," I said.

"He wants help," Big Moms said, smiling at me and winking.

"You shithead," I said to him. "*Kill* you."

He smiled and raised his eyebrows once.

"Just help me," Enrique said, touching my arm. He sniffed at me and said, "Hmm, you tried to use cologne to cover up body odor."

"Sorry."

He quickly said, "No, it works for you."

He rubbed my face a little.

"*And* you shaved," he said. "What the fuck."

I looked at the internet page again and helped Enrique order a pizza.

To order, you had to click on icons of ingredients then move the icons over a steel grater, for them to sprinkle over the pizza icon below.

Enrique pointed at ingredients and I clicked them and brought them over the grater.

Every ingredient, clicked and brought over the grater.

Pieces spraying.

At the top of the webpage there was a picture of the owner's face.

I said, "We should be able to click on his face and drag it over the grater."

"Stop," Enrique said, grabbing my arm again. Then he said, "Ok that's good I guess."

I finished the order, imagining the owner's face dragged over the grater, screaming as pieces of his face sprayed the pizza and the screaming was the "ohhhhhh" kind not the "ahhhhh" kind.

"All right later," I said.

Big Moms said, "Later masturbator"—winking at me and smiling.

"You no-good homo," I said.

Enrique crossed his arms and did a wave from one hip to the other, saying, "Buh."

I left.

Decided to go get a sandwich.

In the hallway, I took out my phone and sent my brother the message: "Remind me to explain 'neck sizzles' to you."

Neck sizzles were something I'd recently done to Rontel.

You just twist the hair on his neck over and over while he falls asleep.

My brother didn't respond until I was almost at the sandwich place.

He sent: "Just saw a video of a baseball pitcher dying when the batter hit the ball right back into his face."

*

I got a sandwich at this place near my apartment.

I didn't like the food there, but felt very hungry and dizzy.

I went in and ordered.

The man put together my sandwich as I directed.

I pointed at the things I wanted.

"That bread, please," I said, pointing towards some bread behind a glass blocker.

It was very intimate.

An intimate process.

A mutual trust.

A marriage.

In which he agreed to gently make my sandwich as I directed.

No, commanded.

The manager started yelling at the customer behind me in line.

"*Vutt kind bread, vutt-kind-bread,*" he yelled.

The customer looked hurt and scared.

Felt like turning to her and saying, "More like, 'what un-kind bread,' eh?'"

And I thought that twice as I was looking at her.

And she noticed me right before I looked away—so it seemed like I was trying to look at her then not get seen.

Just felt terrible, yuh.

The employee making my sandwich said, "Vutt else for you, man dude."

He smiled, gently sliding my sandwich across a cutting board.

The tips of his latex gloves hung off a little.

His latex gloves looked so elegant.

And yes, I was happy to be with him, working together.

I began to use different words for including each ingredient.

I said, "Some onions on there, please."

He said, "Onions, yes yes."

Then, "And, hit me with some tomato."

He said, "Tomato"—gently applying tomato slices with his elegant latex gloves.

"Then slap on some cucumber."

"Cucumber, yes," he said.

A dance song played over the PA.

"Gas it up with some spinach."

"Spinach, yes."

"Yes," I said.

There was another employee next to him, making someone else's sandwich.

The tips of her latex gloves had shriveled.

I said, "Oh man, you got them sizzle tips"—pointing at her gloves by tapping the glass blocker.

It felt weird to have initiated a conversation.

Paralyzed me for a moment.

Weak.

She smiled.

She raised her eyebrows and said, "Vutt."

I pointed at her gloves.

"Your gloves," I said. "That's from bacon, right. You made bacon and then it burnt the tips of your gloves. That would happen to me when I worked at a sandwich place. 'Sizzle tips.'"

She smiled and looked at the gloves and nodded. "Oh, j'yes."

"It hurts, right," I said, smiling for some reason.

"Oh," she said. "J'yes, hoort bad."

"Sizzle tips," I said, then continued interacting with the man putting together my sandwich. "Some spinach and then we're good I think."

"Already spinach, boddy,"

"All right yeah," I said. "That's good."

He had both hands on the cutting board, looking down at the sandwich.

We were almost done, and I think he realized it.

Looked like he wouldn't be able to release this one.

How many sandwiches had he made then been too sad to release.

Or was this the first.

Did I break him.

Did I crush him, tear away his beloved.

As he handed me the wrapped-up sandwich, a customer at the beginning of the line said, "Whatchoo thank, o'boy like me *wouldn't* want some banana peppas onnat shit, put that shit onnat nah. C'mawn, mang." Then he laughed like "heh ah" and put his hands in his pockets, sniffing.

Paying for my food, I imagined myself accepting change from the cashier then floating sideways out of the sandwich place.

Just, out the door and up into the sky.

Not too fast, not too slow.

With enough time to fully enjoy it.

*

When I got home, there was a note underneath the apartment door.

The note was handwritten on lined stationary with flowers and birds on it.

It read: "Hey could you please please please stop smoking. It's stinking up the hallway and it makes me want to vomit. Please, it's bad. Thanks!"

I took the note inside and sat on the couch.

My brother was sleeping on the floor—his shirt off and underneath his head for a pillow with Rontel curled up on his chest.

I read the note again.

It hurt.

Hurt so bad I almost threw my sandwich against the wall.

"*...Thanks!*"

The exclamation point stung.

Neither my brother nor I smoked.

We'd been wrongly accused.

Now wait just a second, hold on there.

Just because there are birds and flowers on your stationary and your handwriting is nice don't mean you can come to my floor and just shit in my mouth.

I'm innocent, muffucker.

Stop shitting in my mouth like this with your damned lies!

I graphically imagined myself stomping someone's face, yelling, "This is *my* floor, muf*fuck*er."

Then I grabbed a red pen off the windowsill and wrote "Die" on the note in big scary letters and put the note halfway underneath the door of my neighbor across the hall, for him to find and worry about, haha!

(Plus I's pretty sure the note was for him.)

*

Without any real effort I'd been able to avoid meeting and knowing a single person in my building except Enrique and Big Moms.

Oh, except the person directly across from me.

Doug.

I always saw Doug coming in and out of the building—usually with a rolled cigarette in his mouth, carrying some kind of motorized bike he'd created from a mountain bike and what looked like a lawnmower engine.

Every time I encountered him he was already saying something, as if we'd been talking.

Like, "Fuckin' has to be here somewhere, fuckin' lost my cellphone you know cuz I borrowed it out, ha."

Or: "So now I have to get a new stroller at the fuckin' flea market."

My only extended interaction with him was one morning, really early.

There was a knock at my door.

It was Doug.

He was talking fast already.

He said, "Oh man, so'm fuckin' trying to pack to go to Boston and shit—me and the kid have to meet the grandparents there—and my wife's already there, fuckin' and I gotta pack and get going but I have to go out and get some things and I don't want to get my kid ready and take him to the store, can you, do you think you could watch him for a little bit while I go out."

I looked at him.

I was trying to think about how many times I'd interacted with him.

Did I know him.

Did I really know anyone.

Just kidding/who gives a shit.

I said, "All right yeah. I'll be over."

And I thought about how low my voice was and how bad my breath was and how that might be scary to a baby—like, just this thing with a deep voice and bad breath, watching over him.

Would the baby internalize the experience as a monster that then followed him throughout life in different forms.

Just kidding/hope so.

Doug looked confused.

He said, "Oh ok, yeah, you can watch him over here I guess. I's going to bring him over, but yeah."

"You were going to bring your baby over here," I said.

Rontel was at my feet with his forehead against my leg, twisting his head over and over.

My neighbor said, "All right man, hurry up and come over. He's a little sweetheart but I gotta get going too so, ha," and he tapped my chest with the back of his hand.

I put on a shirt and pants and went over.

Doug was walking around his apartment, moving shit around, knocking shit over.

He said, "Man, my wife would fuckin' kill me if she knew what this place looked like when I showed it to you, ha, but no, it's fine man."

The crib was in Doug's bedroom.

He showed me into the bedroom and said, "Here, let me introduce you t'is lil shithead here."

The baby immediately looked at me and smiled.

A few months old maybe.

"Aw look at that smile," Doug said, touching the baby's chin. "He's just fuckin witya though."

I thought—This baby is fucking with me.

Doug returned to walking around, looking for something.

I stood by the crib.

A big cat walked past my legs then jumped up on a few things and was next to me, perched on the crib.

The cat stared at me, making a really low purring sound.

From halfway inside a closet, Doug said, "Aw now that shithead wants your attention too. Man, Jesus. It's all about you I guess, ha."

By the crib I noticed a terrarium with newspaper ripped up in it.

"What is this," I said. "What's in the glass thing."

"Tarantula," my neighbor said. "He's cool too. Roy."

I looked at the baby, then the cat, then the glass cage where the tarantula hid.

I thought—These are the days when the tarantula stays hidden.

My neighbor put his head into the doorway to his bedroom and said, "All right man, be right back. Fuck. I gotta get to the grandparents' place, sheez. They wanna see him. They haven't seen him. My wife's Jewish. They're all connected man. Her dad's fucking rich. He has a plane or some shit."

"Oh, a plane," I said, looking at the baby—who'd begun pumping his legs up and down, lying in place on his back.

Hey, you're a baby.

You little baby you.

Who's a little baby, is it you.

"Yeah, a fuckin' plane," Doug said. "All right, be back. He likes that purple duck by you there."

And he left, slamming the door and running down the stairs.

I stood there looking at the baby, then the cat, then petting the cat, then looking at the tarantula cage.

Where am I.

Felt like I just wanted to sleep on the floor and hope nothing bad happened.

I imagined myself getting down onto the floor and saying to myself, "Hope nothing bad happens," then the cat lifts the tarantula out of the cage and feeds it to the baby—lifting the tarantula from its cage, the cat walks over to the crib on his hind legs, blesses the baby with the spider then feeds the spider to the baby, whole, putting his paws over the baby's mouth to make sure the spider is eaten.

This is a cute baby—I thought.

I'll give you that.

There's someone in this room who's a cute baby, and it's not me.

Is it you.

Look at me, tell me, is it you.

I think it is.

I kept smiling at him and he kept smiling at me, pumping his legs up and down, his arms out to the sides in flying motions, lying on his back staring at me.

His hands were in complete fists except the smallest fingers, which he kept extended, and which were very small.

I picked up the stuffed purple duck by the crib and waved it over the baby.

He smiled.

Started laughing and squealing.

He didn't have any teeth.

Just gums.

Look at you—I thought.

You don't have any teeth.

Ridiculous!

The cat kept trying to get my attention too.

"And you," I said. "You're a shithead."

I felt pretty happy.

Had the urge to pick up the cat and get in the crib for my neighbor to find us all angelically asleep together when he returned—but then I was worried I wouldn't be able to sleep and I'd get caught peeking when my neighbor looked in on us.

I petted the cat's head.

He was purring a lot and twisting his head against my palm.

"You silly bitch," I said.

Then focused on waving the purple duck again.

The baby liked it.

He just stared and smiled at it for a long time.

Then his face became serious, and he kept pumping his legs up and down, staring at the purple duck.

The diapers made a sound as he pumped his legs and I created a drumbeat in my head to the rhythm.

I felt at peace with the universe.

No, I didn't feel that.

I pinched the baby's toe.

He kept laughing.

"Your toe feels weird," I said. "Ew, no offense."

Then I couldn't stop laughing.

Uh, is there a little baby anywhere here, I'm looking for a little baby.

Is there a little baby anywhere around here, did you see one.

I'm looking for a little baby.

You little baby.

"Pardon me I'm looking for a cute little baby," I said. "Has anyone seen one. *Any*one."

The cat looked like he was getting ready to jump into the crib.

"Ah, ah," I said, loudly. "Fuck outta here."

The cat meowed and looked at me.

My cat is better than you—I thought.

My cat is the only cat I like—I thought.

Which means, I don't like you.

I stood there feeling so tired, waving the purple duck and pinching the baby.

Every few minutes, I checked the tarantula cage.

One time the tarantula was out, looking at me (seemingly) like, "Ey, fuck you, bitch. I'm Roy."

My neighbor came back fifteen minutes later.

He put some shit away in the kitchen and came into the bedroom carrying a thin tinfoil pie tin.

He held it out and said, "Here man, take this. It's pumpkin pie. My friend made it. Thanks for coming over and helping."

He was paying me in pumpkin pie.

I said thanks and went across the hall.

I locked my door, ate two pieces of the pumpkin pie—holding the pieces in my hand like pizza—then went back behind the bedsheet into my room.

I was thinking something like—My life, it's not terrible, I won't be dramatic, but it's something that, if offered, I'd say, "Nah," and I'd be smiling a little but totally secure in my choice.

*

When I finished my sandwich I went out to look for jobs.

Took the Red Line to Addison and walked around shitty Wrigleyville—with all the bars and restaurants—half looking for dishwashing jobs, half just walking around.

I felt a little happier than usual though because of how much I liked the pants I was wearing.

Recently bought them at the Salvation Army.

They were really good.

They were grey and a little smooth, like sharkskin.

Soft and slick.

Cost me six dollars.

Felt such fulfillment.

Usually when I buy Salvation Army pants, I get home and they almost fit but then there's like, a huge extra area of space (or lack of space) by one knee, or something else random, like tight thighs or something else I'd never think of.

But this pair fit so well.

The way they fit seemed to enclose my genitals and ass so nice as to be sexual.

Felt caressed.

Caressed in foul delight.

Such foul delight.

Oh North America, how I want to show you such foul delight!

*

When I was at the Salvation Army buying the pants, I folded them over my arm and walked around the store for a while—just to delay buying them, to prolong the feeling of anticipation, the sex.

And out from the toy aisle, an overweight homeless man walked up to me, smiling.

He was holding a few board games, each a decade or two old.

He was a foot shorter than me and had a huge stomach that hung out of the bottom of his shirt.

His shirt read:

"I
(image of heart)
America"

Only one side of his top teeth were present—and those angled off to the side, making his head look slanted.

Like his face had collapsed.

Like a house with a wall knocked out.

He had a cartoony voice too.

Made phlegmy sounds.

He pointed at my beard and said, "I yike how y'have dat. I yike ew beewd."

"Oh, thanks," I said.

"When y'have beewd-uh, don't haffa cut ew face in duh mo'nin," he said, and made a shaving motion with the hand not holding boardgames.

Smiling, he still hadn't blinked.

Felt like he was giving me a "naughty" look.

I wanted to shake my finger at him and say, "Don't get naughty with me, man."

Couldn't tell if his eyes were light blue or grey or silver or something else I didn't know.

Couldn't tell if he was looking at me, or slightly above me.

Fuck.

Like he was lifting me off the ground by looking directly at me with one eye and slightly above me with the other.

Holding me up just a little.

Paralyzed.

"Yeah, I hate shaving," I said. "It sucks. I really hate it. I seriously—I hate it so much."

He laughed and got a little closer.

His laughs had a honking-inhalation and/or sniffing-sound at the end.

Like, he laughed then breathed-in through his nose or mouth.

He said, "Beewds mate ew lutt smawter. O'der and smawter."

"Hell yeah," I said. "Thanks. That's nice of you."

He got closer.

Still smiling, still staring.

He made me very uncomfortable.

And I championed him for it.

Nice work.

You're my champion.

He said, "Yeah but when ew come inchoo my do'way at home, I be waiting to hit ew in duh head wit a two by fo," —still smiling, same look on his face.

I laughed, didn't say anything for a moment.

Then I said, "What. Come on, what's this mean stuff now."

He didn't say anything.

Holding his boardgames, belly hanging out.

He adjusted the boardgames and I noticed how small his fingers were.

Such small fingers.

I forgave him for everything he ever did—even his intention to kill me with a 2x4—because of how small his fingers were.

I (heart image) America.

I paid for the pants and walked out of the store, feeling excited about the pants and not even knowing how well they fit yet, wow ahhhh!

I looked back into the store from the sidewalk.

Could see the cartoony homeless guy looking at clothes.

He looked very interested in a hooded sweatshirt featuring a professional football team's logo on the front.

Seemed like the hooded sweatshirt was coming with the boardgames.

Then he walked away.

*

I wore the pants for the first month or two straight—even to sleep—without changing.

Only I eventually did have to change them, because I went twice without underwear after not washing myself post-sex.

Always found you can put your pants in that situation twice before needing to change—before you could smell your genitals through the pants.

Could smell my genitals today, sweating through Wrigleyville.

I decided to go back home after not seeing any signs about jobs (and just generally not wanting to talk to anyone).

I'd gone into one place and asked if they needed help and the guy seemed to say yeah and I was like, "I can wash dishes and shit."

Regretted adding "and shit."

And the man asked for my phone number but it didn't look like he would call me plus there was no way to leave a message on my shitty phone and I was too discouraged to set up a voicemail.

And shit.

Walking through Wrigleyville in the heat, half looking for dish-washing jobs, half just walking.

My brother sent me a message.

Half a minute—gone.

Subtracted.

Twelve and a half minutes remaining.

Death death, the plunge.

Him: "Hey that microwave you mentioned is still here should I grab it."

Me: "I still work?"

"Yeah."

"Should we smash that shit."

Him: "Yeah man."

Subtract subtract subtract.

Minutes gone.

Into the terrible plunge of death, oh lord.

I envisioned myself falling into a deep pit, as seen from above, with my arms out reaching for the place I always already was.

And my life felt complete, satisfying, and worthwhile.

But only for like, twenty seconds.

Kill you—I thought, addressing Chicago (but more accurately, anywhere I was or would be).

*

When I got home, my brother was sitting on the floor drinking water.

His hair was sticking up and he looked unfocused, petting Rontel.

The microwave was on the floor next to them, no sign on it anymore.

"But," I said, "does it still work."

My brother put his water glass down and swallowed loudly.

Staring straight ahead, he made the sign of the cross then slapped Rontel's ear and said, "Let's find out."

Rontel rubbed his face against the microwave.

My brother grabbed Rontel and held him up like a handpuppet.

He put his finger on Rontel's bottom lip and made the bottom lip go up and down, doing fast laughing sounds like, "Meh meh meh meh."

*

I carried the microwave, after my brother asked who was going to carry it then quickly said, "Not me."

In an alley a few blocks away there was an open fence to an apartment building courtyard.

My brother grabbed the microwave from me—yelling, "Yuhhhhhhhhh"—running into the fenced area.

He went up the back staircase.

He was moving fast, considering how he had to hold the microwave in his outstretched arms, away from the rusty back part/broken part (neither of us were updated on our tetanus shots).

Three flights up, he leaned over the railing and checked below.

With both hands—overhead, soccer style—he threw the microwave off the deck and into the alley.

The microwave hit the ground a few feet from me and compressed a little, sending out small pieces.

It was great!

Always felt like, if I could pause time, I'd just go around and break everything then un-pause time, leaving people unharmed but everything else broken, even clouds, mountains, and the sun, maybe a fish or two as well.

*

My brother and I ran home.

We slowed down by the entrance to our building and stood there.

I said, "Why did we run. We could've walked."

"You started and I followed," my brother said. Then he said, "I feel like I'm faster than you, but that you could run for a longer time than me."

I said, "Yeah, definitely."

And I remembered the gum I had in my mouth.

Worried I'd inhale it while catching my breath.

What would that do to me: a piece of gum, stuck in one (both?) of my lungs.

I saw myself decaying in the corner of a room empty but for a toilet—wheezing in the corner, purple-skinned and seconds from death.

My brother gave me the gum a couple days ago and I saved it.

It was pink and had been in a dresser drawer for a long time.

When I ate it today after my sandwich, the gum crumbled into dust at first.

It was extremely hard to keep the pieces together in my mouth but once they all combined it was nice, and then, hey, I was chewing gum.

Regaining my breath out front, I spit the gum against the wall of the apartment building.

The gum bounced off instead of sticking, which is what I imagined it would do, stick.

Why didn't it stick.

Definitely thought it would stick.

This means something—I thought.

Followed my brother into the apartment building.

I thought about inventing a word for when your smile becomes a laugh.

The breaking point between the two.

This is the breaking point—I thought.

And I had a strong urge to tell my brother I loved him because I'd never done that and he'd never done that and he was the only person I talked to so it seemed important.

*

My brother showered and went to see his girlfriend.

I lay on the tile floor, playing with Rontel.

Dripping sweat.

I thought about how tomorrow, I'd completely change my life.

Tomorrow I'd do something new.

Something as yet undone.

Yes.

Tomorrow will be the start.

I'll do something I've never done.

I'll go to the store and purchase a new videogame.

The videogame will be a new release.

I'll say, "Which is the newest, best game," to an employee, then buy whatever suggested.

I'll take the videogame home, reading the instruction manual as I walk, because the anticipation to play the game will be so intense that I'll need to read the manual before I even play.

At home, I'll play the videogame to its conclusion, completing what the game asks of me.

Play the game until I win.

I'll fucking win.

And the winning won't be hard, because the game will have been designed for someone to win with very little trouble.

And early evening will pass into the next day, sun rising on me through the (blinds closed, DUH) windows.

And I'll turn the videogame off.

Stand, stretch, walk to the window, open two blinds with my first and middle finger, and look outside.

No focus, just looking.

Forever, as a feeling that takes place inside of time.

What next—I'll think, staring outside.

What next, Chicago.

How do you want me to fuck you, Chicago.

Then I'll go to bed, to another terrifying dream of being on the deck of a ship during a violent storm.

Same fucking shit.

Sweating on the floor this afternoon, I decided to take a shower to stop sweating on the floor this afternoon.

*

After the shower, I noticed my only towel wasn't clean.

It smelled really bad and had crumbs all over it and I think Rontel pissed on it and it would probably give me a rash.

So I got some paper towels and used them to dry myself off.

At first, looking at the sheets of paper towel, I thought—This is the saddest thing that will ever happen to me.

But no.

That's silly.

Using paper towels to dry off after showering might not be bad.

Why get upset.

Why get upset about anything.

Everything felt automatic.

Controlled.

Control yourself.

Ok, I will.

No, you don't even know how to start.

That's true.

Look at the paper towels.

Dry yourself.

It's a new day.

Start this new day.

You can do anything you want, just have to dry off with those paper towels first.

Exciting.

Exciting because I knew if I wanted, it could be the beginning of a new period in my life.

One where I solved problems as they happened.

One where I solved problems before they even had all their elements.

A new period where I eliminated problems before they were problems.

With no fears or concerns, because those were for people who viewed life as a future, not something already happening.

A period where I thought, "No future"—and meant it positively.

A period where I stood up and said, "Yes, I have used paper towels to dry myself off after showering, and I don't care if I do it again and again—except for the cost of buying the paper towels."

This is it—I thought, standing in my bathroom naked and dripping, already sweating again.

This is all there is.

Nothing else outside of being here right now, naked and dripping.

Sweating.

No end to the recycling.

Just keep going keep going.

Stop thinking.

I began to dry myself off.

Noticed you can't use the same drying motion with paper towels as you can with a fabric towel.

Truly, two different towels.

The best method was to fold two connected paper towels in half—over each other—then gently touch them down over the wet areas of your body.

Scrubbing motions wrinkled and tore the paper towels.

I was able to dry off my whole body with about three paper towels, adding a third to the first two near the end.

In conclusion, using paper towels to dry off: not bad!

It was a nice, fun way to keep dry.

Something new.

Also, it kind of made me feel like an escaped prisoner, or someone running from someone else maybe, maybe some kind of secret government agency.

Like I'd broken into someone's apartment and had to use whatever was available then quickly escape.

Have to get out quick—I thought, smiling.

Have to escape.

I thought about escaping as I dried off.

Then I thought—No, this is all there is.

Can't get out.

Rontel came into the bathroom and licked water off my shin then drank water from the faucet in the bathtub.

He sat under the faucet sticking his tongue out to each drip.

Timed.

And I folded the paper towels and threw them on the floor.

On top of all the old hair and beard clippings from when I'd cut my hair or beard without sweeping.

But yeah, paper towels.

Not bad!

*

After that, I went to the Uptown Public Library to use their air conditioning and internet.

It was difficult for me to always use the Uptown Public Library for their air conditioning and internet because of the hatred I felt towards the place for never responding to my job application—the one I partially completed then just submitted, hoping it wouldn't matter that certain parts weren't complete.

But, I'd been using the Uptown Public Library internet to visit this website that sold a lot of different products and allowed you to write reviews.

I'd write reviews for random products.

Today I did one for paper towels.

I titled the review: "We all know paper towels are a whiz in the kitchen," and then the review went, "But did you ever think they'd be so great to dry yourself off, like after a shower or day at the beach!? I say—*beep beep*—go ahead. These little numbers are perfect for just, getting ready for the day. And they're so much more portable than a bath towel. I can now carry like, six squares with me at all times and be able to shower/swim no matter what situation I'm in. And, I, LOVE, swimMING! Not sure you can even begin to appreciate that kind of freedom unless you invest in a package of these bad boys!"

Then I changed "bad boys" to "babies."

Then back to "bad boys."

I gave the paper towels four stars out of five.

After reviewing the paper towels, I found a product no one had reviewed.

Earplugs.

I wrote this review: "Wow, just…disappointing."

Then realized I was writing the review about myself.

Then realized every negative thing I'd ever said was about me too.

Ouch ouch ouch.

Stinging!

I did another review, for a twenty pound barbell.

The review was: "So, ok. I'm a fitness FREAK! But this barbell just isn't doing it for me. Nope, no way, Jose. I think it's going to take a much MUCH bigger barbell to successfully smash my mother's head in. Bottom line: Great for fitness though. Definitely feel stronger."

In the review section for a television stand, I wrote a review titled: "This is actually a review of my girlfriend's roommate."

And the review was: "Well I went into our relationship (me and the roommate) wanting to be nice. Not friends, just nice. You can't expect to be friends with someone. That doesn't happen. That's what my girlfriend doesn't understand. It can't just be like, 'Now we're friends.' It just happens. IF IT HAPPENS. So I wanted to be nice. I wasn't going to do anything more or less than I would for anyone else. Anyway, I'm not one for the bullshit :) so I'll just say it: Roommate = TOTAL MEANY!!! I tried to be nice. But she just ignored me. Wouldn't respond to anything. I'd say hi and she wouldn't say hi back. And I never fucking say hi, so, shit. Need I say more? TOTAL MEANY!!! One out of five stars (and I'm being nice here, folks)."

Then I deleted "folks."

Then I typed it again and left it.

Seemed like I was yelling, "Fuck you" in my head the whole time—maybe my whole life.

Sitting in the Uptown Public Library.

The person next to me at the table had a nectarine out.

I had the urge to say, "Want someone to be my FRIEND

here!"—slamming my balled fist down on the nectarine as I yelled "FRIEND."

*

On the way home, I stopped at a corner store and bought an 18 pack of soap.

In line at the store I looked at the 18 pack and felt relief.

That's 18 bars—I thought.

That will last a long time.

Shit, *each bar* will last a long time.

Think about 18 of them.

When it's all over, I'll be a different person.

A completely different person—unrecognizable as any past version.

It was calming to me to know that many things would happen before I needed to buy more soap.

Who knows if I even will have to buy more soap.

Maybe something will happen.

Maybe someone will give me soap.

Maybe I'll die.

Maybe soap won't even be used anymore.

Maybe a meteor will destroy earth.

Maybe I won't even care about soap anymore.

I looked at the 18 pack.

Relief.

I walked home with it in my arms, confident and happy.

Relieved.

At home I stacked the bars in the bathroom cabinet.

It is time to begin using the 18 pack—I thought.

Now is the time to begin.

I smiled.

I was already different.

Sent my brother a phone message: "Hey there's 18 bars of soap here now if you want some."

Eventually he sent back: "Who gives a shit."

I sent back: "Just leave me a few bars you know."

*

That night when I left for my girlfriend's, the Wilson Street Red Line stop was barricaded on all sides.

I walked up to the barricade.

Police cars.

Ambulances.

Firetrucks.

ATF units.

Riot shields.

Weapons.

People standing around watching.

Uncle Sam came up to me, in the middle of saying something about the hotdog he was eating,

Uncle Sam was a homeless guy in the area.

I called him Uncle Sam because he wore this American flag top hat.

He also wore sandals with sweatpants and a suit jacket over that.

Our relationship began after I met him out front of a grocery store where he was asking for change and he asked me to buy him a chicken dinner from the store and I bought the chicken dinner for him and we became, I think, friends.

The only time I asked him his name he told me it was "Bob-Fred."

Two first names hyphenated.

That's how he said it.

Tonight he approached in a strange walk that involved lifting his knees up abnormally high, his face doing odd twitches as he put condiments on a hotdog, everything backlit by police and emergency lights.

It was beautiful to watch Uncle Sam walk through the light.

He was beautiful.

"Luh me a hotdog," he said, twitching.

I said, "Yeah," squinting at the light.

Uncle Sam told me it was a hostage situation and then explained to me the way he likes to eat a hotdog, applying condiments to the one in his hand.

He said, "Dude like me, I'm pu'n spirals on a hamburger, and fo a hotdog, I wind em back and forth."

"Double-helix style," I said, suddenly wanting to ask him so many questions.

He looked at me.

He pointed at me with the fingers holding the mustard packet, and said, "S'a double hee-liss style, yuh."

He rubbed his twitching face against the shoulder of his suit coat and made a weird motion with his lips, like he'd just put on a new face over his skull and was aligning the lips with the teeth.

Behind us, someone who'd been evacuated from the train explained what happened, on her cellphone.

A prisoner, in transport to another jail, killed two police officers and escaped the bus and got on the Red Line and got off at the Wilson stop, then killed someone and took someone else hostage to the rooftop of a nearby apartment building.

Police and civilian death.

Uncle Sam continued putting condiments on his hotdog.

He said, "Jesus luh you no matter what you do. Yuh yuh. But you can't get into heaven with nunna them acka-hol and cigrets, oh no."

Then he took many small bites of the hotdog without chewing each bite, leaving only 1/3 of the hotdog.

He squeezed mustard from the shriveled packet onto the end of the hotdog, like he was painting.

Full-mouthed, he said, "Yuh. Dude like me want mustard on eyr-bite. Bah-zam! Blam a lam. Dude like me want mustard each and eyr bite, yuh. And you caint get inta heaven wit nunna them acka-hol and cigrets doe."

"Good shit," I said. "So the train's not running."

He swallowed and laughed, stamping his feet.

He said, "Muh fucka keewd a cop, now they keew him, watch." Uncle Sam pointed at the rooftop with his mustard packet. "Man, send me in thuh. I fuck s'ass up. Cuh Jesus luh you no matter what."

"Me and you," I said. "We both go in, we both come out."

I held out my hand.

"Yuh," he said, moving the hotdog towards my extended hand as a sign he'd shake my hand if his hand was free.

I said, "All right, I'm going to the liquor store to get a phone card for my shitty ass phone."

"Yuh," he said.

"Or maybe not, should I just throw this phone against the ground," I said. "How about that."

"Yuh," he said, laughing. "Jesus luh you no matter what."

He was smiling, face twitching.

I took out my phone and threw it—with authority—against the ground.

The phone broke apart.

Uncle Sam laughed and put his face to the inside of his elbow and repeatedly made a motion with the hand holding the hotdog, as if he were throwing the hotdog like a paper airplane.

There were news channels everywhere.

Helicopters.

"He gon surrender," said Uncle Sam. "Muh-fuckiss always surrender."

And he seemed so disappointed, like he'd seen this before.

Like maybe just once it'd be nice to see no surrender.

I said, "Only pussies surrender, man."

Uncle Sam laughed.

He coughed harshly, bending at the knees a little.

Top hat waving just a little with each cough.

No, don't die.

He pointed at me with the last bite of hotdog.

He said, "You cold."

I said, "Fucking right."

"Co-dest," he said, laughing.

And for some reason I imagined our severed heads connected by a glowing double helix—floating up to the apartment rooftop where our vibrating power stopped the violence—and everyone cheered us, the two headed double helix, as we went to other planets to help likewise, yuh, travelling the world helping people.

No/who cares.

Behind us, a drunk woman walked up and started making sounds at the hostage situation.

She had on a dirty NFL winter coat.

Uncle Sam's woman.

She stood there toothless, making noises at the situation.

Like, not words, just noises.

Then she came up behind Uncle Sam and slapped his head hard and said, "That's not only *your* cigarette, gammee it."

Uncle Sam ate the last of the hotdog and held up his empty hands and said, "S'a fucking ha-dawg, bitch."

*

So I had to run over to my girlfriend's.

It was five and a half miles.

I liked running over.

It was cheaper and faster than the train too.

In fact, fuck the train and fuck Chicago and fuck each United State.

I went home and put shorts on and lay on the floor, sweating, vowing—to myself if no one else—to figure out a way to kill everyone in Chicago.

"They all have to die," I said, looking across the floor at Rontel, as he lay there blinking, streetlight across his face through the blinds in sharp lines.

*

I walked the first couple blocks to prepare my legs.

Had to wear boots because my other shoes fell apart.

It was almost dark out, but still over ninety degrees.

One street before Clark St., a raccoon walked around someone's front yard.

And a dog walked out from the backyard, approaching the raccoon.

When I rounded the corner, I heard the dog whimper and shriek loudly.

And I started running with a smile on my face—thinking something like, “These are the days when the dog loses to the raccoon.”

And that made me smile even more.

To be my own stupid best friend.

Let me show you how a real man accepts the weights of shrieking terror.

*

On the run over, I thought some more about my “Talking to yourself is…” stationary.

I’d been thinking about creating this personalized notepad or like, calendar, or something similar, where on each page at the top it had, “Talking to yourself is…” then at the bottom it had something unique.

But so far, I’d only come up with like, ten ideas.

I had:

Talking to yourself is… “the result of having no one to talk to, even though there are plenty of people to talk to.”

Talking to yourself is… “never avoiding the argument.”

Talking to yourself is… “killing a strong animal such as a gorilla or rhino using only strikes to the mouth with your fist.”

Talking to yourself is… “killing a strong animal such as a gorilla or rhino using only your mind/kindness.”

Talking to yourself is… “being too worried about people knowing your thoughts.”

Talking to yourself is… “feeling comfortable.”

Talking to yourself is… “keeping a small animal frozen (having been frozen alive) in your freezer.”

Talking to yourself is… “not changing your shower curtain in so long that when you were showering the other day and saw a fly emerge from a moldy fold in the curtain, you were convinced fly larvae grew there (and it probably does).”

Talking to yourself is… “one thousand years of numb-handed surgery.”

Talking to yourself is… “too many cookies and not enough milk.”

And the run was nice.

But I felt depressed, thinking how sometimes the hardest person to talk to you is yourself.

Just, nothing to say.

Kept thinking there was so much to say.

But there wasn't.

Didn't have anything to say.

*

Running over a bridge on Damen St., I heard song lyrics in my head, from this dance song they played at the sandwich place earlier.

The lyrics were, "End of the world/end of the world/wake up, wake up/it's partying time."

At first I didn't like it.

Thought it was dumb.

Thought it was just another dance song.

But then I thought about the lyrics.

The lyrics made a lot of sense.

I appreciated them.

Like, all right, if I was sleeping, and it was the end of the world, I'd want someone to wake me up.

I'd also want to know if it were partying time.

Wouldn't want to have to say, "Hey, what time is it," only for someone to have to then tell me, "It's partying time."

Because if it WASN'T partying time, I might not want to be woken up.

But if it WAS partying time—and I was asleep, like in the song—then I'd want someone to wake me up and tell me.

If someone woke me up and just stood there, I'd say, "Why did you wake me up, I was sleeping."

So whoever wakes me up should say, "It's partying time," maybe while pointing both thumbs over one shoulder to indicate where to go for the partying.

And oh how I'd smile and shake my head and be ready to start partying (after I woke up a little, and maybe stretched).

*

When I got to my girlfriend's apartment, she'd already been asleep and I got in bed with her—resting, but unable to sleep.

I lay there until the sun began to rise, hosting an endless trail of interconnected and unresolved thoughts.

Thought about this homeless woman I saw in a grocery store parking lot last week.

A hundred degrees out and she was wearing a big fur coat.

And her weave went sideways as she bent over and slowly chased an injured seagull.

The seagull looked weird—like a crawling pile of hair—because of how it moved in sideways hops, one wing bent and extended.

Sideways hops.

The homeless woman followed each sideways hop but never closed the distance.

Hopping sideways, the injured seagull.

Looking exactly like the woman's weave.

I wanted to see her weave jump off her head and land somewhere by the broken-winged seagull, then both hop different ways.

And the homeless woman in the fur coat—wearing only the hairnet now—can't decide which to follow.

She screams to the sky.

And for some reason in the sky I saw boxer James "Lights Out" Toney staring back down at her and the injured seagull.

I started thinking about Toney vs. Holyfield, one of my favorite boxing matches.

Midway through the second round, when James Toney began winning, he'd put his hands down and dodge a punch by moving his head back then thrust his head forward and stick his tongue out, dodging the next punch.

Then later he'd gesture to the ringside judges after every punch he landed.

He'd gesture to the judges and ask them to make sure they saw the punch.

The fight ended in the ninth round when Holyfield's corner threw in the towel.

Right after the fight, when security and family and promoters entered into the ring, James Toney went to Holyfield's corner and hugged him and said, "I luh you, man" a number of times.

Then Toney returned to his corner to have his gloves removed, tape cut off his hands.

He started yelling at the camera.

He said, "Detroit. Detroit, baby. Ypsi. Ypsi, baby, Detroit. Y-town, y'know wh'I'm talking bout. This how do it when you from the D. This how do it in the D, man. Ain't nobody do it like this. I put a, I put a—" he looked to the side, pointing his finger downward, "—I put anotha southern brotha in the ground, man. They cain deal wit me. Nobody can deal with me."

Then a broadcaster approached Toney and tried to interview him.

The broadcaster said, "James, were you simply too quick tonight."

Toney said, "I'm too quick fuh anybody. Cain nobody hang wit me in the heavyweight d'vision. Assa bottom line." And he got agitated, addressed the broadcaster by name. "I'on't know, Jim. Don't try-uh come up here, give me no bad-ass questions, try-uh degrade me wi' some—"

The broadcaster moved the microphone to his own mouth and said, "Question's legitimate," then moved the microphone back to Toney's mouth.

Toney said, "Holyfield's a great fighter. Don't diminish zat—enny time." Then he grabbed at the microphone a little, to hold it. He said, "He a warrior, an'he came to fight. Bottom line."

The broadcaster moved the microphone back to his own mouth to say something but James Toney leaned forward and yelled, "Who nex. I got milk baby. *Nex!* Uh, my mom, Sherry, Uncle Larry, all, everybody, I luh y'all."

He kept yelling but the broadcaster took the microphone back to his own mouth and said, "Did he ever hurt you at any point tonight."

Microphone back to Toney's mouth where he finished saying, "Cousin Scott, Auntie Janina, everybody, luh y'all. NEX!" Then he wiped sweat off his face with a towel and, very calmly and quietly—almost hurt—he said, "Nah he'ain never hurt me, man. I'm undestructable, man. Don't forget. When I'm ready, I'm undestructable. I fight ennyone, ennytime."

He took a deep breath then yelled, "Nex!" thrusting his head toward the camera. Then he paused, took a deep breath and said, "Nex. Who nex."

Someone from his entourage said, "Detroit, baby."

Toney yelled, "Detroit, Ypsi, Ann Arbor, I'on't care."

The broadcaster tried to say something but Toney kept talking.

He said, "Whoever my promoter tell me, 'at's who I'm knockin ova next. D'troit." Hitting one hand into the other, he said, "Ey, ey, ey man, bottom line, my talent speak fuh itself. I ain got answer no one else's queshuns, I'm going home. Have a pawdy. We goan have a pawdy. And eyr-body that doubted me—" he paused, made a serious face right by the camera, "—or didn't respect me—" paused again, "—fuck em."

He turned his head to the side.

A guy from his crew said, "You got cho respect, baby. You got it."

Toney passed by the microphone again and said, "Scuse me."

The broadcaster tried to say something else, but Toney kept talking.

"Ey, bottom line, Holyfield's a great fighter," he said, "I watched him when I's kid. I did what I had to do. I get paid to do. Bottom line, Detroit inna house." Then, addressing someone through the camera, he made a phone gesture with his thumb up to his ear and his pinky finger up to his mouth. He said, "Ey baby. Ey bay, I got ya message, baby."

The broadcaster put the microphone under his own mouth and said, "James, James, let's try to have a decent conversation or interview here. Hold on a second."

Toney started yelling again.

He took the microphone out of the broadcaster's hand and threw it down.

Then he backed up, staring at the broadcaster, saying something inaudible.

Someone handed the broadcaster the microphone again and sound returned.

Toney stared at the broadcaster.

"Don't run up on me, dog," Toney said. "I'on't like that."

And his entourage took him away.

But he returned to hug Holyfield before Holyfield's interview and Toney said, "Ey, I luh you man,"—then he let go of the hug and slapped Holyfield's shoulder. "Much respect to you man. Much luh."

My girlfriend took a deep breath and made a noise then turned over, facing me.

For some reason I was passingly terrified she'd have James Toney's head/face.

Like, her body, with Toney's head and face.

And then of course, she'd open her eyes quickly and lick me, making the 'thup' sound too, ew!

I got milk baby.

Nex!

Who nex.

It was hot in my girlfriend's room and I couldn't sleep and I'd never sleep again.

Fuck everything except me.

*

Fell asleep for an hour or so and the first thing I heard when I woke up—already sweating, already feeling sick—was some drunk guy on the street, yelling, "There you are! Thought you was hiding, eh!?"

I wanted to yell, "You'll never get me!"

But I had a headache and my mouth was dry.

I sat up, looked out the window at part of the Chicago skyline.

Kill you—I thought.

My girlfriend was already out of bed, in the bathroom.

Today we were supposed to go to this one-day beekeeping class.

She asked me to come with her a while ago, and I said yes.

So today I was going to a beekeeping class.

*

We stopped at a grocery store on the way.

Everyone had to bring something to eat.

"What should we get," my girlfriend said. "Should we get fruit, or a pie, or."

"Let's just bring a lot of gum," I said. "And a single bottle of shampoo."

"Think I'm going to get a blueberry pie," she said, extending her neck as if to see where the pie was in the store. "You know? Fuck it, that's good right."

"Fuck it, here's your pie. Take it, fuckers."

"Exactly."

"It'd be funny if we brought it in and like, a big part of it was already eaten," I said. "Plus, I'd like to do that because I'm very hungry right now."

She said, "Yeah" but didn't look like she meant "Yeah."

She went to get the pie and I wandered around.

*

In aisle four there was a scuffed-up, barely-thawed hotdog on the tile.

This is it—I thought.

This is the saddest thing ever.

Can't get any worse than this.

Escape.

I had to escape.

It was traumatic.

I left the aisle.

But after wandering, I wanted to return to the aisle of the hotdog.

So I did.

And when I got back, two girls exited the aisle, stepping around the hotdog.

They had disgusted looks on their faces.

One said, "That. Is terrible."

The other said, "Ew, I stepped on it and it rolled a little, ew."

They both laughed.

I went to find my girlfriend.

Wanted to tell her about the hotdog development.

She was in line waiting to pay.

The line was long so again I returned to the aisle of the hotdog.

What haven't I learned—I thought.

I stood at the end of the aisle with the hotdog.

A woman pushed her cart towards us.

Here it comes—I thought.

This is it.

Having returned to the aisle of the hotdog, I accept this fate.

The woman rolled over the hotdog with her cart, unknowing.

And the hotdog crumbled some more.

And I felt insane, trying not to laugh as I got back in line with my girlfriend.

To pay and leave.

*

At the bee class, everyone grouped in a small multipurpose room, putting food on a table.

I looked at the different foods on the table and considered walking up to each, eating some so everyone could see, then loudly denouncing the quality of the food, saying, "Next," as I walked on.

A fifty-year-old man came up as I set our pie on the table.

He wore khaki pants and a dress shirt underneath a pale yellow sweater.

He had eyeglasses and his hair was combed to the side.

He set two quiches on the table.

"Got a vegetarian one," he said. "And, for you carnivores, this one has sausage."

He looked at me and the pie I had set down.

He said, "Some people like hot pie, some like cold pie. I, personally, love it."

Then he didn't say which he personally loved.

And I wanted to know!

His name tag had "Bill" on it.

"You're Bill," I said, and shook his hand with both hands and held the shake for a long time.

"Well," he said, smiling a fake smile, "How long've you wanted to know about bees."

"Ever since I can remember," I said, putting my hands in my pockets, lightly touching my testicles with my left hand.

He said, "Oh."

"Yeah since my youth, basically," I said.

People began sitting for the class.

Bill sat with us.

He and my girlfriend talked—because excited and polite people find and keep each other.

Bill talked quietly, but with amazing enthusiasm.

He seemed to be "fascinated" by a lot.

Many of the things my girlfriend said left him "fascinated."

When Bill asked my girlfriend what she did for a living, she said, "I teach tenth grade chemistry." She said it as if for a moment she didn't know if she did or not.

Bill said, "Oh fascinating. That's cool. I think everyone should know more chemistry."

And he meant it.

My girlfriend said, "Yeah, science is cool."

I said, "How much spinach can you make with science."

Lately I'd been using "spinach" to refer to money.

"*So* much spinach," she said.

The tone of her voice suggested she didn't enjoy my company right then.

What a shame!

"So, with science," I said, "basically, you get that spinach."

"My wife has magnificent spinach in her garden," Bill said. "It really is a lovely thing."

I said, "Oh, she got that spinach?"

The beekeeping instructor began trying to use the microphone and someone said the volume made her ears feel "absolutely awful" so the instructor said he wouldn't use the microphone but then someone else introduced herself alongside her mother and said her mother couldn't hear well, and the bee instructor asked the mother if he should use the microphone and she smiled and nodded—not hearing what he'd said—and the daughter said, "Just go without the microphone, it doesn't matter," and he stepped away from the microphone and began the lecture.

*

Shortly after he began, I considered raising my hand and saying, "Yeah, I can kick your ass," while leaning back in my chair—maybe then look around at others to see what they thought about that.

Maybe point at someone and raise my eyebrows, "You," getting off my chair, letting it hit the floor loudly, "you think anything about that."

And everyone would know then I could kick his/her/anyone's ass.

The instructor delivered a long speech about beekeeping and I drew pictures on my complimentary beekeeping packet.

The instructor seemed very worried the whole time.

I kept expecting him—after everything he explained—to say, "But I mean, who gives a shit, right," and then look around shrugging and doing this laugh that's more like sniffing.

Some of the phrases I heard while drawing pictures on my complimentary beekeeping packet:

"...which is a very gentle time in a honeybee's life."

"...can anyone speak to that: apple-scab spraying."

"...he's a third-generation Bosnian beekeeper."

"...I get stung about once a week, although sometimes I won't get stung for three or four weeks then I'll get stung four or five times at once (sniffing laughter)."

I stopped drawing and pictured him out working with bees—getting stung—saying, "Ow"—getting stung again—saying, "Ow"—getting swarmed—screaming—and his scream is the scream of a person you don't think matches how he looks.

*

One of the people attending the class kept asking questions and/or introducing himself to the conversation.

He kept referencing having lived in Hawaii.

I wrote, "He's from Hawaii," next to some drawings in my bee packet.

Then I tapped my girlfriend on the shoulder and tapped the pen against the words.

She read it and nodded.

I wrote, "I want to fuck your hot pussy," and tapped her.

She read it and said, "Shh," smiling.

Then I wrote, "Sorry for being such an asshole sometimes, I care about you," and tapped her, but she didn't look.

Hawaiian guy was still talking.

Hawaiian guy was really intense and earnest.

Everyone was really earnest.

Made me think.

What was wrong with me.

Why couldn't I get excited about something like beekeeping.

Get really excited.

Just come to the class today and enjoy it.

Why couldn't I live like that.

Viewing almost everything with excitement/enjoyment.

Why couldn't I just enjoy something.

Why instead did I always envision my own corpse, smileless and rotten.

Smileless and rotten.

Just, terrible.

At the end of our table there was an overweight kid who'd been making faces at me the whole class.

He held up a picture he drew—of a horse—and crossed his eyes at me.

I thought about holding up a piece of paper that read, "Fuck you, bitch"—and raising my eyebrows up and down a few times.

Another person at the class was American Wilderness.

In the back sat a concerned-looking man wearing an "American Wilderness" sweatshirt, who began to dominate the question-asking.

His sweatshirt had "American Wilderness" airbrushed on the front—over an airbrushed bear, which was over an airbrushed American flag, which was waving.

American Wilderness kept asking questions, with a very stern look on his face, his hands gesturing as if opening a combination lock.

I imagined him eating a cookie—only he wasn't wearing the American Wilderness sweatshirt, he was shirtless.

And cookie crumbs fell into his dense chest hair, dissolving.

Almost every question he asked was—according to the bee instructor—"Going to be addressed later."

*

When all the questions were done, the bee instructor showed some slides of poorly maintained bee boxes.

He showed slides of all the ways someone can ruin a beehive.

The last slides were bee boxes destroyed on purpose.

He said, "And—I guess—here's some random vandalism from teenagers."

Everyone said, "Ohh," and seemed upset.

I thought—These...these are my bees.

*

On break, Bill told us he'd already ordered his bees.

The bees had to be ordered from somewhere.

Bill said, "They told me to call the post office to let them know they're coming."

He was talking to my girlfriend, but I said, "That's a scary thing to call someone and tell them. 'My bees are coming.'"

He looked at me for maybe six seconds and said, "Right yeah."

My girlfriend said, "That's exciting, that they're already on their way. I'm jealous."

Bill said, "Oh I know, I'm just falling in love with bees."

And he really was falling in love with bees.

My girlfriend was too.

They were two people who loved everything.

And excited and polite people who love everything find and keep each other.

*

When break ended, the instructor went around the room and asked each person to introduce him/herself then state his/her reason for taking the class.

Bill had his legs crossed, hands clasped with fingers together around the knees.

He said, “Well, I’m Bill and I guess I’m just—and I was telling these guys earlier—I’m really just, falling in love with bees to be honest.”

Everyone said, “Ah,” or, “Uh huh,” or, “(agree in some way).”

Another person introduced himself and said he too had always been fascinated by beekeeping.

Then he referenced living in Hawaii numerous times in astounding succession.

Hawaii Man again.

When it was my turn, I said, “I’m here because my girlfriend asked me to come with her and said she’d pay, and also because I want to control nature.”

The overweight kid at the end of the table said, “Control nature!?” really loud and crossed his eyes then held up a game of tic tac toe he’d drawn on his bee packet.

When it was his turn to introduce himself, he got real nervous and said, “Um yes, hello, I’m Eli. I like bees uh, because um, because they’re my favorite thing to love because I like them and I’m an artist.”

Then the next person began her introduction.

Eli made a face at me, biting a muffin he’d acquired during break.

Fuck you, bitch.

*

After the beekeeping class my girlfriend and I went to a secondhand store in Humboldt Park.

She wanted to buy clothes and make them into different clothes.

She walked around looking at clothes and I walked around feeling like I wanted to hit my head against something and hurt myself.

My skin warmed up and felt hardened.

Felt like I couldn't comfortably be inside any building.

Wanted to leave.

From behind a rack of clothing, someone said, "I'm sayin', all they shorts is fuck-TUP, Darryl."

Then Darryl said, "You sayin' they *all* bogus. Well I'on't want none then. Fuck this."

In the main aisle, a kid stood in a shopping cart.

We stared at each other.

Will he fall.

Face smashed on the floor.

Me standing there.

Inevitably someone would walk up and see me standing there with the kid lying facedown on the floor, blood coming out around his head.

What would be the normal thing to do in that situation.

Do you say hi to the first person who finds you or do you just shrug or do you start to help or what.

My girlfriend stood at the end of an aisle in front of a small cracked mirror, holding some clothes up against her.

"What about this," she said. "I kind of like it."

I focused on breathing.

I purposely didn't look at anyone.

Just me calmly and openly accepting my role in this equation.

Which always equaled a loosely defined sum.

Which always equaled just slightly more than itself.

"It's nice, I like it," I said, touching my finger to the shirt she held. "I love it more than anything in my life."

"Even me," she said.

I looked at the shirt then back at her face.

Neither of us said anything as she continued to hold the shirt up against herself.

She said, "I think I like it, yeah."

And I moved some shirts along a rack in front of me.

There was one with Osama Bin Laden's face on the front, a big red X through it.

Underneath his picture it said, “America doesn’t back down.”

And, in reference to nothing, I thought—I’ll never back down, motherfucker.

Didn’t matter what because I’d NEVER back down.

And that felt good.

My girlfriend held the same piece of clothing, doing this odd series of poses with it, almost like a dance.

I looked up and saw a sign hanging from the ceiling.

It had two columns, indicating the location of things.

It listed things like “Men” and “Boys” and “Girls.”

One of the things listed was “Hot Styles.”

I wanted to walk up to an employee and say, “Excuse me, could you tell me where the hot styles are. Oh, nevermind, there they are.”

Why would anyone want anything other than hot styles.

Who would see that there are hot styles, and then not just immediately go there.

I envisioned a sign I’d make for the store.

And the sign was bigger.

And it only had “HOT STYLES” written on it in big letters.

And there were arrows all around it, pointing out at all areas in the store.

I stood behind my girlfriend, staring at myself in the mirror.

I repeatedly thought—Hot styles/these are hot styles here—until I felt calm.

Girlfriend said, “How about this one—no?”

I said, “These are some hot styles.”

“The hottest styles,” she said.

I said, “I’m looking around and it’s just, all hot styles.”

She didn’t say anything.

She kept repeating this cycle of poses in front of the mirror.

I said, “I want you to call me ‘Hot Styles’ from now on. Call me that or I won’t answer, ok.”

The kid who was standing in the shopping cart rolled by, his mom pushing.

Still standing, staring at me like I was hot styles.

*

My girlfriend looked through the aisles of plastic and glass objects and I walked around.

A man came up to me from one of the clothing aisles.

He had on Velcro shoes, sweatpants, and a huge white t-shirt.

His hair was long and greasy and he wore swimming goggles.

Kept doing this series of mouth tics.

Twitches.

He'd draw his lips inward, then extend them, making his mouth into an *o*, and then say, "Ohp."

He did that eight or nine times before he said actual words.

Eventually he asked me about winter coats.

It was so hot outside—and had been, and would be—that people were dying.

But I helped him look for winter coats.

There were none.

"No more winter coats," I said.

He kept saying, "Ohp," over and over, a little more nervous/upset now.

I tried to explain.

Tried to tell him.

He just looked sad, repeating, "Ohp," over and over.

Soon as I started backing away, he said, "Ow."

Started saying, "Ow," and just stood there between aisles.

And it seemed like he understood everything—or if not everything, then at least some amount of things that a person like myself might easily confuse for everything.

Amen.

Amen, brotha.

Hot styles.

Triumph.

Triumph of the hot styles.

Hottest style wins.

This is the beginning—I thought.

This is the beginning of a new period in my life.

One where I solved problems as they happen.

Where nothing happens.

I joined my girlfriend in line waiting to pay.

I openly grabbed her ass and said, "Hot styles."

People at the next cash register were talking.

One described to the other a commercial she liked and what happens in the commercial and have you seen it?

*

My girlfriend took me to get pie, because at the secondhand store I made a comment about not getting any pie at the bee class and she thought I was genuinely upset and I didn't try to change her mind.

We went to her "favorite pie place."

We walked from the secondhand store.

She turned to me after a considerable silence and said, "Hey, did you smell that one guy back there."

"The homeless guy," I said.

"Yeah."

"Yeah why," I said.

"He smelled *so* bad."

"He's fucking homeless, of course he smells."

She didn't say anything.

"What's the point of saying something like that," I said. "Why would you even fucking say that."

She didn't answer.

We continued walking.

No conversation.

A few blocks later, someone behind us yelled, "Kevin," repeatedly.

I started to think he thought I was Kevin, and he was trying to get me to turn around.

What if I really am Kevin—I thought, and just never knew it.

But I forced myself to not turn around.

If I turned around to confirm who he was yelling at, he might continue to think I was Kevin.

And if he thought I was Kevin, I'd have to answer for not turning around initially.

I'd have to answer for forgetting my own name.

*

By a small four way intersection, there was a group of teenaged kids.

One of them blew on a kazoo loudly.

As we neared, he stopped.

I was worried he was going to blow the kazoo right as I walked by—startling me for everyone to laugh at.

Everyone fuck off, I'm not Kevin, and I don't want to be frightened.

A crackhead with only her two brown front teeth walked by us quickly, yelling, "Need a dolla fo'hotdog."

She seemed to be yelling to anyone—like, as a precaution against not asking someone who would if asked.

I silently tried to manipulate my girlfriend into buying me a hotdog, in addition to the pie, and my method was looking at her and squinting my eyes.

*

We sat across from each other at the pie place.

Our table looked out at Milwaukee Avenue.

My girlfriend read through a weekly Chicago newspaper, making comments about every bar/restaurant listed.

"Ohhh we should go here," she said, pointing at some picture of a plate of food with an address and review beneath.

"No," I said. "I don't like going places. No places for me. Never again after this."

"Ohhhh, this place," she said, looking up at me. "This place has the BEHHHST fucking green beans."

"Best green beans, muffucker," I said. "You wannem, well, here they are, muffucker, my greenest beans."

I decided to just repeat everything she said.

Because we weren't having a conversation.

She was just referencing things she bought or wanted to buy.

Most of our interactions were like that—her describing something she bought or wanted to buy.

So I'd just repeat what she said and add "muffucker" to make it seem like I was encouraging her, make it seem like I was in a good mood.

"Whoa-bob, this place has aMAZing scones," she said, tapping a description of a restaurant and making a noise with her mouth.

"Boy you know we got the best scones, muffucker," I said. Then I grabbed a corner of the newspaper and ripped it and said, "MufFUCKa".

"Motherfucker," she said, with passive disapproval, straightening the rip.

A pie store employee walked past us.

She made eye contact with me and smiled.

I'm too goodlooking—I thought, gravely.

Goddamnit.

The employee locked the entrance and said, "Take your time, I'm just closing up."

My girlfriend and I sat there eating our pie.

Most of my life could be characterized as "being somewhere/doing something with someone who has paid to ensure I come along."

The other part of my life could be characterized as "not."

My girlfriend said, "Oh I forgot to tell you, my sister's pregnant."

I listened to her talk about her pregnant sister.

But I was thinking about dogs.

I want a German Shepherd—I thought.

And I imagined myself dressed in some type of ceremonial robe, standing with both my arms out, palms upward.

And above one palm floats the fully-enclosed fetus of my girlfriend's sister's future baby, and above the other palm floats the fully-enclosed fetus of my future German Shepherd.

And my face is emotionless.

And above my head there's a fire but it's clear and just looks like the air is waving.

I stared out the window watching things happen on Milwaukee

Avenue, eating pie with my girlfriend.

2012.

Living.

What happened to me.

Outside, someone walked up to the pie store and tried to come in.

When he noticed it was locked he looked at the store hours.

Saw it was closed and made a face, looking downward at the sidewalk.

Then he looked up.

We made eye contact.

Maintaining eye contact, I picked up my plate and took a big bite of the pie and made a face like the pie was too good to endure—leaning back a little as I chewed, closing my eyes and touching at my throat and face like a woman nearing orgasm.

He laughed and gave me the middle finger before walking away—hands in pockets, looking down at the sidewalk.

*

We waited for a bus out front.

My girlfriend called her sister, leaning against the bus sign.

I paced.

The first thing I heard was, "Hey, how're things!"

And I thought about how I'd answer.

I'd answer that things weren't working for me.

That there were only things.

And I couldn't get them to work together.

Other things would indicate, "No, we're not going to work with these things."

I'd make like, two or three things work then realize those two or three things were attached to everything else, which never worked, which stopped referencing each other and became just things.

And I'd be helpless again—standing there with things in front of me.

A pile of things, piling more but only ever making one pile.

A life.

Born with it, though felt like something that never happened.

Not a phase.

Not something to get over.

But something to overlook, to forget about.

Something that's there.

I stood sweating on the street with vague and unguided thoughts about being an architect who knows nothing, but tries, learning what not to do the next time—each next time having less and less energy to produce anything.

A series of accidents creating exactly the same thing, resulting in the same sad person, everything connected to time as it happens, without any ability to turn around and stop it even for a second to say "what is happening" because that is happening.

And eventually your body just learns to operate so slowly it looks like you stop moving and decay—looks like you die—but you don't.

Everything else around you just speeds up and learns to look different until you look dead by comparison.

But it always makes sense.

Never any errors.

Of course.

Of course this is what's happening—I thought, standing on Milwaukee Avenue waiting for the bus.

And it felt like things were going to have meaning again maybe.

Also felt like I couldn't imagine anything that would make me feel better.

I walked up behind my girlfriend and lightly kneed the back of her knee and she fell a little then breathed in quickly, saying, "Ahhh."

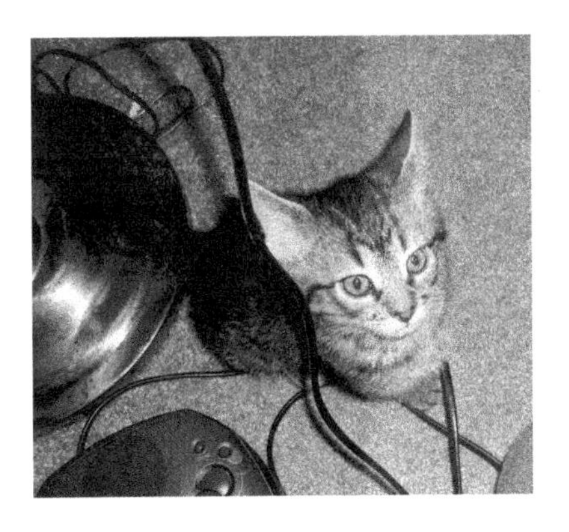

ABOUT THE CAT

Rontel is three years old. He lives in Chicago.